Marks Dunlee dozed, but it seemed that he had hardly closed his eyes when one of the most bloodcurdling screams he had ever heard shattered the night air. In an instant the longhorns sprang to their feet, snorting, bellowing, and milling in an uneasy mass. Marks and the other drovers put on their hats and scrambled to their horses.

A great fear laid its grip on the men. Any second that tossing sea of beef could crash like a tidal wave through the night. And in this terrain of ridges and plains that most of the riders did not know, anything could happen.

Nobody seemed to know who had screamed—or why. . .

LONGHORNS NORTH

JIM ROSS

LIVING BOOKS
Tyndale House Publishers, Inc.
Wheaton, Illinois

Cover illustration by Paul Turnbaugh

First printing, May 1987

Library of Congress Catalog Card Number 86-51482
ISBN 0-8423-3815-2
Printed in the United States of America

LONGHORNS NORTH

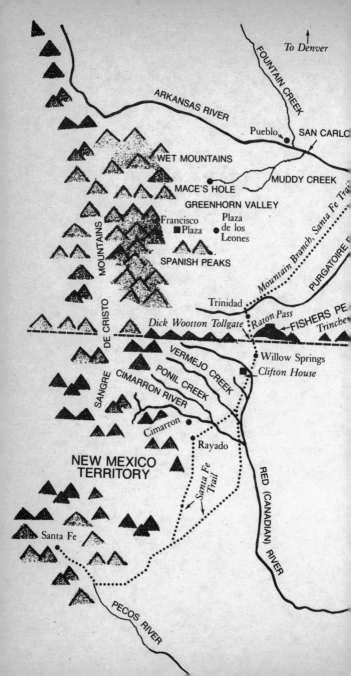

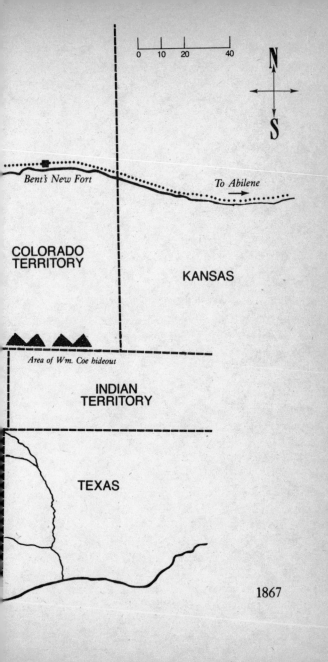

0 10 20 40

N

S

Bent's New Fort

To Abilene

COLORADO
TERRITORY

KANSAS

Area of Wm. Coe hideout

INDIAN
TERRITORY

TEXAS

1867

Historical Note

This story carries on the Dunlee family saga. It is set in 1867, shortly after *Ambush at Vermejo*, and seven years before *Treachery at Cimarron*. Texan Marks Dunlee is seventeen. Lonan and Shad, his brothers, have minor roles. Several characters in *Ambush* reappear here. Frank and Jeanie Spellman are at their Cimarron ranch. The towering outlaw, Wile Gaster, who fought with Lonan in *Ambush*, now rides the right trail.

Many historical people of the West are here. Lucien Maxwell of Cimarron, sometimes called the Southwest's greatest land grant baron of the period around 1845–1870, is in the background. Others are Uncle Dick Wootton, famous mountain man and trader who ran a tollgate in the Raton Mountains; Tom Stockton, who built a ranchers' rendezvous, hotel, and stage stop known as the Clifton house on the Canadian (Red) River; Alexander (Zan) Hicklin of the Greenhorn Ranch, one of Colorado's most colorful figures during the Civil War and until his death in 1874; Peter Dotson, who had been a U.S. marshal in Salt Lake City but by 1867 ran a ranch near the mountain valley that rustlers use in *Longhorns North*; Robert Fisher, trapper and trader whose favorite mountain valley was named "Fisher's Hole" for him; Juan Mace, whom many claim drove rustled cattle into that valley, whence it became known as "Mace's Hole"; John Heffner, who trained Confederate recruits at "Mace's Hole" while Union cavalry searched for the Rebel hideout; and Tom Tobin, uncanny tracker who traced the notorious Espinosas to their hideout camp in 1863.

Other historical figures who appear in the novel are John Iliff, biggest Colorado cattleman of the 1860s, whom the famous trail drover and rancher Charley Goodnight dubbed the squarest man on the plains; some of the earliest pioneers of "Mace's Hole" (now known as Beulah, Colorado), such as the John Jacob Pease family and the Professor John Boggs family; Jim Gray, who operated a ranch stage stop a few miles northeast of Trinidad, Colorado, in the 1860s; John Dawson, a rancher northeast of Cimarron; Smith Sayers and his wife, settlers at Willow Springs which today is Raton, New Mexico; John Thatcher, who was a famous businessman and leader in early Pueblo and has descendants still in business there; George Stout, proprietor of the Valley House in Pueblo, where Dodge City stage coaches pulled up; William (Cyrus) Coe, outlaw chief of 1867-68; Madison Emory, who lived in the area not far from the Coe gang's stone fortress, Robbers' Roost; and Charlie Dodge and Jim Reynolds, outlaws in Colorado in the early 1860s.

Also in the background are famous landmarks, such as Fishers Peak (Cimarron Peak to many old-timers) in the Ratons, the two Spanish Peaks, the Purgatoire River in southeast Colorado, the Plaza de los Leones (named after Miguel Leones but later named Walsenburg after Fred Walsen in the 1870s), Fort Francisco or Francisco

Plaza built by John Francisco, Henry Daigre, and Hiram Vasquez, the Culebra range west of Walsenburg and La Veta, the Greenhorn Mountains a bit to the north, the Wet Mountain range still farther north, and the black volcanic plug called Huerfano ("Orphan") Butte a few miles northeast of Walsenburg.

I hope my readers will enjoy this novel set within the Colorado and New Mexico territories.

Jim Ross

1

From a ridge near the South Canadian, Marks Dunlee gazed across the Cimarron rangeland. He folded the worn map that drover Frank Spellman had sketched in Texas.

"When you come with my cattle," Spellman had drawled as he pointed the way on his map, "just follow the Horsehead Crossing route that Charley Goodnight blazed last year. Stick with the Pecos to Fort Sumner. After that, swing west and then north with the Canadian. Pass what they call the 'Wagon Mound' rock upcropping here an' cross this fork where one branch of the Santa Fe Trail cuts its ruts away to Rayado. Trail the critters on north an' you'll strike Ponil Creek. It'll lead you northwest to my cabin."

Then Spellman and his riders had headed north along the Shawnee Trail to Abilene in Kansas Territory, taking a herd he already had. He'd gathered longhorns from brush thickets in southwest Texas. They roamed there wild by the thousands at the close of the War Between the States, and they bore no man's brand.

Spellman had left the map with one of Goodnight's friends near Fort Belknap on the Brazos River. As he'd asked, it had been passed on to Shaddo Dunlee. Shaddo had rushed home to the Dunlee ranch when news reached him that robbers had stolen money from his ma. His brother Lonan had already lit out on the trail of the robbers, taking his seventeen-year-old brother Marks.

Then the father, Tom "Buckskin" Dunlee, had come home from a wagon trip to take care of the home front. Lonan sent Marks back with the body of Uncle Jack, who had been ambushed along the trail. Shaddo and Marks then joined other drovers to deliver the cattle to Spellman's ranch near Cimarron in New Mexico Territory. As ramrod of the drovers, Shaddo took the map and asked Marks to scout ahead with him for bedding grounds and Indian signs.

Marks's eyes swept out over a prairie of tall, sun-yellowed grama grass. Far to the west hulked the majestic blue peaks of the Sangre de Cristo, a part of the long Rocky Mountain chain. Reaching from the foothills toward the east were ridges like giant fingers garbed with piñon, juniper, grass, and rock. Vast grassy valleys lay between these, gutted by flowing creeks and dry arroyo beds that slashed southeastward. Far off in one of the lush meadows Marks could see a small herd of buffalo grazing.

A smile of satisfaction crossed the square jaws of the tall, lean-hipped drover. Spellman's FS ranch house and corrals could not be further away than three hours, even at a herd's slow pace.

"Lonan." He whispered his brother's name on the soft breeze. He'd see his brother at the FS ranch. A few days ago, close by the Pecos, a Texas outfit returning home from New Mexico Territory had carried the news. Lonan Dunlee had shown up at Cimarron trailing the robber and killer. He'd helped spring Spellman free from an outlaw hideout and found cattle that rustlers had taken from the FS.

Lonan had caught up with the killer he'd trailed north from the Brazos, then along the Arkansas River westward to Bent's old fort, and south to Cimarron. He'd sent word along that he'd strike out for Texas after he helped Spellman through the fall roundup.

Shaddo lay sprawled in the carpet of grass behind Marks. His posture showed his heavy weariness. Once he'd taken a look at the trail route to the northwest, he sank down to relax for a few minutes. Being trail boss of this outfit had been a punishing grind day and night. And, like Goodnight, he was possessed of an iron will to get the cattle to grass, water, and past lurking Comanches, Apaches, and Utes.

Suddenly Marks snapped fully erect from a nonchalant lounge against a slab of granite. He swung up the field glasses and riveted a probing gaze on a strip of range. It lay out there to the north and a bit east, painted by patches of high brush and junipers.

Comanches or Utes? He and Shad had spotted a small party of Ute braves a half hour to the south. But it was a downcast group that would pose no threat as they struggled toward Cimarron off to the northwest, where they would get rations of beef, flour, and blankets.

Now Marks caught a flicker of movement again. The glasses fixed on the area. Not far off a mouse-colored mustang, a grulla, was slapping hard through brush, tearing at breakneck speed. A slender rider hugged the dark mane that whipped in the wind. The rider's free hand lashed the grulla furiously with a quirt. And the rider was a woman.

Had Indians jumped her?

She shot over the range as if fired from an army howitzer. Another horse and rider burst out of the brush a stone's throw behind. The second horseman was bent on overtaking the woman. Tall in the saddle, he rammed brutal spurs to his claybank but was losing ground to the grulla.

Marks flung a sharp yell to Shaddo. It fetched the trail boss from his catnap like the urgent summons of a cavalry bugle.

"Trouble!" Marks yelled. "Two riders! Man chasin' a woman!" He dug hard for his long-legged sorrel, spur rowels singing.

"Man chasin' a woman," Shaddo murmured. "Huh! Nothin' new!" But he shoved on his dusty black hat, snatched up his Winchester rifle, then blistered a path to his bay.

Hitting his saddle, Marks caught the blur of his older brother hauling his bay around. The two drovers scrambled to the top of the ridge and spotted the girl again.

Marks gave the sorrel free rein to tear down the slope as fast as he could without piling up. Then he spun the mount squarely in the path of the girl and flung up a hand for her to stop. She hauled back on the reins and brought the bluish gray horse to a halt that sprayed sand.

Marks saw that she had a pretty face. But he could not be sure of the wild look on that face. Surprise—or fear?

"You in trouble, Miss?" he yelled as Shaddo pounded over. The girl started to reply, as if eager, but her voice choked up. Her face, drained of color, was set in a frame of dark hair that cascaded down in shiny strands out of a

16

dusty white Stetson. And as her grulla danced nervously and she struggled to control it, Marks saw a bad rip in the side of her gray, woolen blouse.

"I—I was trying to . . ." Her words were a labored croak from a parched throat. Marks did not catch what she said at the end. Her answer was lost under a thunder of hooves as the rider on the girl's trail galloped up and savagely jerked his claybank to a grinding halt beside her.

"What you hornin' in for?" His lips curled back viciously from his teeth. Marks had heard the same sentiment in a lobo's snarl before a death slash to a young calf.

"Hornin' in?" Shaddo queried. His eyes narrowed, his lips drew taut, and the strong brace of his jaw thrust forward. He pushed back in his saddle, his right hand near his gun butt. Somewhere on the slope he'd already loosened the rawhide thong that held it in the holster. "We rode down to help the lady. 'Peared she wanted to get away from you."

The girl had dropped her head toward her bosom. The brim of her hat hid all of her countenance save a proud, pert chin.

"Stranger," the man on the claybank scowled with impatience, "you didn't see straight. We was havin' us a race. She got the jump, then this horse stumbled an' fell behind." His glance seized the girl. "Ain't that right? Tell 'em!"

She looked up, swallowed, bit her lip, and shuddered. She seemed cowed by the man. Her words were sickly. "That . . . that's right."

Marks, searching her, wished her eyes would meet his. He knew her voice was weak, quivering, strained. It rang all hollow. Mystery hovered over this meeting not far from the Ponil.

"Mister," Shaddo drawled, sarcasm thick in his voice, "this isn't the best strip to lay out a horse race." A strong arm swept toward the rugged terrain behind the riders. It was choked here and there with tall brush that could punish and slow a horse, and gouged with gullies where torrents had brawled. "They tell me the places for horse races are over at Cimarron. The baron o' this country, Lucien Maxwell, has some o' the fastest horses. Or you can find takers back at the Clifton House they say Tom Stockton has been buildin'."

"The race is our business." The rider's voice was as sharp as a mule skinner's lash. "You better keep outta it. Don't tell us how to run our business."

Shaddo and Marks felt their stomachs tighten. The man was touchy, biting, hostile. He dug into his shirt pocket, dragged out a Bull Durham pouch, and tapped the makings into brown paper. Glaring, he twisted up a smoke and licked it while the others waited him out. Marks's sorrel blew through his nostrils, the grulla under the girl stomped, and a prairie dog scolded from a town not far off.

The tear in the girl's blouse nagged at Marks. And it had not evaded the careful eyes of Shaddo, who received his name because of his skill at shadowing many a trail. Men said he could track a grasshopper through brush, and he seemed to see everything. He noticed that the stirrups of the man's saddle were far too short for his legs, yet the stirrups of the girl's saddle dipped beyond the reach of her boots.

"I never hankered to poke in other folks' matters," Shaddo said in a casual drawl, "but I've been around. Those stirrups—do you ride with 'em that short? An'

18

Miss," he touched his hat brim in respect, "do you like your stirrups outside your reach thataway?"

He'd said right out, in matter-of-fact frankness, what Marks also thought. Yet Marks sensed that the words would not please the arrogant rider. Big brother Shaddo could be blunt as the butt of his Colt .44.

The pursuer blew smoke over the claybank's mane. The gentle zephyr snatched it and its curls vanished quickly. Now he drew himself taut. His sun-darkened face stiffened, and his wolf-green eyes betrayed being caught off-guard. Then his eyes blazed like flame that a gust whips up in dry kindling. His left hand pawed his Stetson back. He ran fingers through a heavy thatch of straw gold hair. His right hand, which had given the reins a dally around the horn, prowled high on his thigh. He flicked the rawhide cord loose behind the hammer. A pearl-handled Colt .44 lurked in slick leather, deadlier than a rattler in its hole.

Shaddo's vigilant eyes had read the sign on the butt of that hog leg. Several notches, chipped out, tallied with the menace of the blond. He was a gunfighter, cocksure, itching to prove his hand.

"Ain't those smart words!" the gunman sneered. "You bound to make me look bad, mister?" His eyes leveled on Shaddo, but the Texan met the stare with unflinching eyes. "Well, as it happens, Miss Voni here jumped on *my* horse. He's fast, so she figgered she'd beat me for once."

"Oh," Shaddo said, as if the explanation cleared up the whole matter. "Get kind of a hollow victory, eh? Miss, is that how it was? 'Course, if it isn't that way, just give us the word. We can set it right."

The gunman sucked in air between bared fangs. He savored the words the way a man likes mesquite thorns jabbed in his ribs.

"Mister," Shaddo spoke up again, "we're waitin' for the lady's answer. An' if that hand strays any closer to that gun, it'll be a mistake—your last. Fair warnin', an' I don't speak idly."

The rider emitted another hissing sneer. Then he broke into a cackle. Cool contempt rode that laugh. "You! You talk that way to *me?*" His words were overlaid by disbelief. "Name's Lacy Tontam. When I fetch a hand to this gun, I make things last. Foller me?"

"We've heard the name Tontam," Marks put in cooly. "Heard of others like it too. They aren't around anymore. This here's Shad Dunlee. Me, I'm Marks Dunlee. An' it's like my brother said."

At this exchange of names, Tontam kicked on his brake. The name "Tontam" had not cowed these riders from the south. Their gaze was firm as flint, eyeball to eyeball. Other men had let their eyes slide away. Something Tontam read in the gaze of Shaddo's eyes ticked a warning. The name "Dunlee" yanked the rope on a bell of caution deep in the gunman's brain. "Dunlee"—a name with which to reckon. Stories had drifted north from Texas, and recently from the Cimarron area, about a Lonan Dunlee, stories told around campfires. Tontam's fingers slid farther from the pearl grip, then the thumb hooked in his belt.

"Now, little lady," Shaddo said, "tell us if you need ary help—ary atall." Shaddo never took his warning eyes off Tontam's. And remembering he'd helped train his brother, he was confident Marks's eyes didn't wander either.

Tontam shifted in his saddle and rasped at the girl. "Go ahead. Tell 'em. It *was* jest a race!"

She recoiled from his voice, trembling. Then she partially looked up, her brim half-masking her face still.

"That . . . that's what it was. Just a race." Her voice was weak. "I just had to beat him!" Tontam had fixed her in the vise of a brutal stare, and she saw. "It's all right."

Marks did not believe that. But she had said it. Just then the dull thud of hooves in sand reached their ears. A voice called.

"What is it, Tontam?"

The gunslinger twisted in his saddle. He peered back at a tall man with broad shoulders and thick torso, pointing a big gray roan toward them at a walk. A pistol was in the newcomer's hand, and it was raised high, ready for action. The Dunlees noted that the man was in a dark gray shirt with an expensive red cowhair vest, a broad-brimmed Stetson, and black pants. He sat in his saddle with the confident air of a king looking down from his throne. They figured him to be in his late forties.

"It's all under control," Tontam shot back stiffly. Then, as the new rider reined up, Tontam jerked a thumb and said, "This here's Hu Scovil, cattle buyer." The girl slumped a bit lower in her saddle.

"So! You've met Voni, my niece." Scovil's voice was gruff, but it rang with authority.

"Yeah," Tontam threw in quickly. "They saw her tryin' to beat me on the grulla."

"Hmmmm. They did? Well, no horse catches the grulla. She's full of games." Scovil smiled wryly, then snorted in contempt. "No harm done. Lucky the grulla didn't fall an' spill her in one of these arroyos. Now, who do we have the pleasure of meetin'?"

The Texas drovers introduced themselves.

"Dunlee, huh? Heard that name. You wouldn't be the Dunlees of Texas that run cattle? An' the Dunlee that cleaned out those outlaws at Cimarron a couple weeks back? Well, well. We're all a long way from home. I'm here from north of the Arkansas River. Came to buy a herd from Frank Spellman. He's got a herd trailin' up from Texas on Goodnight's trail."

"Yeah," Shaddo replied. "We're due at the Spellman ranch. His herd is back a ways. See you there. Miss, a pleasure." He tipped his hat. "Tontam, I can't say as much for you. You'll need to learn your manners."

Tontam recoiled to lash back. Words growled up in his throat. "Anytime you wanta try to teach me." But the Dunlees had wheeled their horses, loping off to the southwest to skirt the shoulder of the ridge and return to the herd. The gunman's words, muffled by drumming hooves, fell into a guttural rasp deep within him.

"Now, what was all that about?" Scovil demanded.

"That," Tontam sizzled, "was a score. A score I'll settle. Some day soon."

"Settle your private matters on your own," Scovil barked from his throne, searing Tontam with his eyes. "On the Spellman ranch, an' till we're a long way from it, mind your manners. Mind 'em good!"

Tontam flicked his cigarette stub into the dust, chewed his lower lip, and shrugged into a dark sulk. Inside, a rage flamed like a spreading range fire.

2

The fall roundup was finished when Frank Spellman laid proud eyes on the fifteen hundred tall longhorns from the Texas thickets.

He already had five hundred other longhorns. Out of these two thousand animals, he'd let Hu Scovil pick fifteen hundred. His neighbor, Hack Griner, would furnish five hundred more for a herd of two thousand to trek north into Colorado Territory. That would leave Spellman with five hundred stocking his ranch.

Other local cattlemen had cut their bunches from the roundup and driven them homeward, men like Lucien Maxwell, Tom Stockton, and John Dawson. Griner held more than five hundred in his herd nearby, and Spellman's herd from the roundup was kept in a long grassy meadow west of his headquarters. The Texas herd that had just come grazed in good grass a short way south of the buildings and corrals.

Now the rancher, new to the Maxwell country in 1867, hooked a boot heel on the lowest aspen pole of his corral. He glinted at the newly arrived cattle in the distance. Shaddo, Lonan, and Marks Dunlee gloried with him in his elation.

"Yeah, you're gettin' a good start," Shaddo said. He whittled a cottonwood chip to form a new stopper that would fit the mouth of his gourd canteen.

"That's a fact," Lonan nodded. "One trip with the two thousand to Abilene this spring and summer. We got back that herd money the ambushers swiped at Vermejo Creek. Now, with your fifteen hundred goin' north near Pike's Peak country, along with Griner's five hundred, you'll really get established."

"Makes a man thankful," Spellman said with a smile. He felt his shoulder. It was still a bit sore from the gun wound ambushers had inflicted at the Vermejo ambush scarcely three weeks earlier. "Folk put me down for dead when Duke had me chained in that outlaw hole. An' many of my cattle had disappeared. But Lonan, you, Josh, and Hack Griner got to the bottom of the plot. You saved my bacon. You saw how glad the wife an' Jackie were to have me back alive."

Marks shook his head, amazed. He'd heard the story. Lonan and Spellman's twenty-year-old ranch hand Joshua Root had come across the rustled cattle in a mesa basin. Later, Lonan led men in a rescue of Spellman. He took the rancher out of the clutch of a gang headed by Spellman's brother, Duke Maskill.

Lonan had shot Maskill. The outlaw chief plunged to his death in the jaws of a hungry mountain lion Maskill kept in a deep pit. Lonan also had recovered money stolen from Spellman on his way home from the Abilene cattle sale. Besides, he'd gotten back the money stolen from his own ma and taken the robber to jail.

Now Spellman, only recently back from Abilene, was back at home on his ranch. His wife and daughter, who had come in a wagon train from Kentucky just at the time he was ambushed, were settling into their pioneer home near Cimarron.

Spellman, before leaving Texas for Abilene, had hired men to stay and gather more cattle running wild without owners. Now he was gratified to see his second herd safe from the perilous Pecos River trail.

"Great to have the buyer get here at the same time," the rancher drawled. "He'll be back from Cimarron tonight, start looking over the cattle tomorrow. Once he's made his pick, we can head 'em north in two, three days. They'll get to their new home before the winter snows get bad."

Spellman gripped the top aspen pole as he watched Longhorns graze off to the south. "Matt Scovil's a good friend. Knew him years ago. Now he has a spread a long way north of Pueblo, east of Fountain Creek. It's the Box Double S, a ways south of the big range of John Iliff."

Lonan nodded. Everyone knew of Iliff, the man who had gotten water rights for many miles along the Platte River. Known as one of the fairest, squarest men on the plains, he'd built a cattle empire selling beef to miners of the Pike's Peak region, army posts, railroad workers, and eastern buyers. Matt Scovil, too, had gotten a hold in this business, and was just as honest.

"Matt lost a lot of cattle in Cheyenne and Kiowa raids since Colonel John Chivington's cavalry massacred hundreds of Indians at their villages on Sand Creek in 1864. They were striking back. Lost others to rustlers that hit him like Juan Mace used to a few years back. Matt's wantin' to restock two thousand head. Figures he can fatten 'em on good grass, then sell at top price."

"A man could take your FS brand," said Shaddo, "an' change it easy to a box with two S's inside." He sketched it on the ground with the tip of a cottonwood stick.

"Exactly," replied Spellman. "Bring the top of the bottom bar on the F down and around to form the lower part of an S, draw a box around both S's, an' let the back of the F form part of the left side for the box."

"It's good to see your ranch growing," Lonan said. He chuckled. "But if you don't watch it, you'll be right up with Lucien Maxwell, running so many cattle."

"No danger," Spellman laughed. " 'Don Lucien,' as the Mexican herders call him, will continue to be the biggest stock man. Rest of us are smaller, but doin' well. Tom Stockton, who's been puttin' up the Clifton House, John Dawson, Hack Griner, an' a few miles south near Rayado, Shoat Hartman—they're all doin' fine.

"Anyhow, this drive will fetch money to buy more cattle nearby, from Maxwell, or from herds like Goodnight's that will come up from Horsehead Crossing. And I promised the wife I'd haul some nice furniture from St. Louis. Been her dream all these years, an' now I hope to make it come true. Besides, we want to help Jackie an' Josh. They plan to get married just before Christmas. Josh wants his own ranch now, an' Griner gave his word he'd sell to them."

Marks felt good about this. Only this morning Josh had climbed on a stagecoach to make connections at Trinidad's Davis and Barraclough office for the Abraham Jacobs line to Pueblo. He was on his way farther north to Denver on some business for Spellman and for himself. He'd be back in about two weeks, maybe even join the trail outfit on its ride back south after delivering the herd to Scovil.

"So the drive north is really important to Mrs. Spellman and Jackie," Marks mused. "I hope they see their dreams realized, like Pa did for Ma. I can't forget the light that came into Ma's eyes when she saw the nice things come off the wagon. I only talked with Josh a few minutes, but I could tell he's pure quill, a man to ride the river with."

He felt a strong hankering to go on with the trail outfit that would take the longhorns north. He'd get a kick out of helping fulfill the hopes of these sterling folk. But Lonan had spoken. Marks was to ride back with him to Texas. Shaddo would go on along the mountain branch of the Santa Fe Trail past Trinidad and Bent's old fort and eastward to Abilene. A man at the new cattle railhead owed money to "Buckskin" Dunlee. Shaddo aimed to collect it.

Jackie came out with a basket to gather clothing from a line near the ranch house. Seventeen like Marks, the dark-haired girl was a beauty. It was rare to see a young white woman in the sparsely settled ranching areas Marks had known. Marks sauntered over, helped gather the clothes, and they chatted pleasantly.

"Like to help me pick flowers for the supper table?" Jackie asked. Marks beamed. He was lonely, and he knew she would be lonely too, even though Josh had only been gone a day.

When Mrs. Spellman called the men for supper, Marks noted something. Voni Scovil came from a back bedroom where she had been resting. Free of her hat, her black hair tumbled past her shoulders, framing an attractive face. Her large eyes could send a cowboy into tongue-tied stammering. Her lips were soft, fresh as ripe plums. Her cheeks curved down in graceful rosiness to a proud chin. When she turned a fleeting smile toward him, he decided that she might turn out to be very nice, maybe as nice as Jackie.

But mystery was still there. He thought he detected fear in her eyes. She gave it away in the furtive way she glanced at her burly uncle.

Hu Scovil and his swaggering bodyguard, Tontam, pushed in to sit on either side of Voni. Scovil sat next to Spellman, who sat at the end of the table. The Dunlees sat on the other side, Lonan closest to Spellman, then Shaddo, finally Marks. The youngest Dunlee found himself right across from Jackie. Jeanie Spellman was at the end opposite her husband. Their loving eyes rested on each other often.

Both Jeanie and Jackie arose from time to time to pour coffee or fetch more food. Spellman did not follow the tradition some did in this territory where many Mexicans lived. It had women eat separately from men when guests were present. At Spellman's table, unlike Lucien Maxwell's at his big mansion in Cimarron, men and women sat at one meal.

The roast beef, potatoes and brown gravy, cornbread with butter, and garden greens made a fine meal that would "stick to a person's ribs." Then the ladies brought on pie baked with wild plums from along the Ponil. Marks had not tasted anything close to this in a long time.

Spellman, Scovil, and Lonan did most of the talking. But Spellman graciously drew his wife and daughter into things at times. Marks was struck by the clear spirit of love and mutual encouragement. It sparkled in this closely knit family. He felt drawn to each of the three. They made him think of his own folks.

Shocking news came from the talk. Matt Scovil, Voni's pa, had been bushwhacked, hit in the back. He had nearly died. But a rugged constitution, a fighting spirit, and the help of the good Lord had rallied him. He was recovering well now, though still laid-up and weak. But his brother Hu, who was visiting him, had taken over the running of the ranch. So Hu had insisted on making the buying trip. He would see that the cattle came to his grassland.

Voni, too, had come along to represent her pa. Her uncle and she would pay one third cash down on two thousand head. First, Hu would pick out the prime animals, and ranch hands would cut them out. Then Hu and Voni would be on their way with Tontam, and a trail crew would take the longhorns north. The Scovils had business at Trinidad along the way home, but they planned to visit the drovers on the trail.

Marks took note of Voni as her uncle talked. Most of the time her head was down. She kept busy eating and said nothing except when spoken to. Despite her graciousness when she did speak, Marks sensed a brooding spirit. Some burden weighted her down. He recalled her torn blouse.

Supper ended and they got up from the table. In the buzz, Voni volunteered to help wash the dishes. But Jackie had her mother's attention at that moment, and while Jeanie heard Voni and smiled, she did not reply immediately. Marks's observing eye caught something. Uncle Hu spun quickly and shook his head at Voni. The girl winced as if a bee had stung her. Then Scovil nodded her off to one side and impressed some point on her in a very low tone. The upshot was that Voni excused herself, claiming she wanted to help but was overcome by weariness. Her uncle felt it better that she rest in her room. Then he followed the men out to the yard.

Marks sauntered out to a bench beneath a cottonwood at the east end of the cabin. He strode near the back corner of the house, gazing at the stars that seemed to be pasted on a ceiling in the sky. Then he heard the voice. It was a man's voice, coming from the room to which Voni has retired. Scovil had gone back inside to speak with the girl. Voni had opened the window to admit the freshness of a breeze, and the words cast a loop on Marks's attention.

"Forget that! You do what *I* say! You don't go along, you know what'll happen! I already made that clear." Scovil's rasp was freighted with mean threat.

"Yes, you did make it clear. But—"

"No 'buts'! I meant every word. See that you remember—and remember good!" Other words followed, but Marks was unable to make them out. Then he heard boot heels thud on the plank floor. The door closed and heavy steps moved away from the bedroom. Marks started to turn. He felt ashamed of listening. Then he heard Voni sobbing.

Marks wondered about the girl. Maybe Voni did not want to return to her home in the company of her Uncle Hu and the ominous Tontam. Then she'd have to ride alone, no doubt on a stagecoach. That might be dangerous. But Marks quickly gave up that theory. The stage company men would watch after a lone lady. Anyway, the tone in Scovil's voice was frightening, brutal. It did not show concern for Voni's safety. It was an outright threat of something cruel.

But he was her uncle, and Marks was only seventeen. What right did he have to butt in, or mention anything to others? He realized that he might be misconstruing the whole thing.

In the two days that followed, Marks and his brothers helped separate the cattle Hu Scovil pointed out. Gradually men of the outfit and some from the Texas drive that had stayed on filled out the two thousand head to go to Matt Scovil's Box Double S.

One of the FS cowboys reined over by Marks near the bank of a broad arroyo and gave his lineback dun a short breather.

"Smiley Landon, that's me," the cowboy said. He flashed a winning smile. "Yo're one o' the Dunlees from Texas."

"Yes, name's Marks. Actually Daniel. 'Marks' is just a tag they put on me."

" 'Marks' it is, then. Unusual name."

"Short for 'Marksman,' " Dunlee replied. "People always wonder about that."

"Oh, you shoot good, huh?"

"Well, I . . ."

"It's OK. I asked. Man doesn't like to brag, but I'd like to know."

"Well, they were having a shoot down by the Conchos River. Some Texas Rangers, some cavalry men, and the best among the cattlemen. The top two were shootin' it off with rifles when I rode in with my brother Shaddo. Before I knew it, some of the cattle crowd started sayin' there was a kid that could outshoot both of them. They pushed me forward, and there I was in the shoot myself."

Smiley hooked a leg over his saddlehorn, grinned, and ran fingers through his long blond hair. "Well, what then?"

"Well, guess I had a good day."

"'Marksman,' huh? You won?"

"Yeah. I took the Henry rifle I carried on my saddle, and put all three bullets inside the three holes of the best of the two men. The brothers said I had become the best shot in the family."

Smiley whistled, then laughed. "Hoot, man. I wish I could've seen that!" He cast a glance wistfully toward the far-off ranch house. "Tell me, Marksman, you've been in on the feasts of Mrs. Spellman. How's . . . well, uh, how's Miss Voni?"

Marks was taken aback. He ran fingers through his horse's mane. "Miss Voni?" Smiley peered at him intently. "You speak like you know the lady."

"Yes. I shore do. An' Miss Voni *is* a lady." Smiley drew a sleeve across a perspiring brow. "A few months ago I left Iliff's big ranch an' rode for the Box Double S. Worked for Voni's pa. Like Iliff, Scovil's a fine man. But I notice Matt Scovil didn't come to look at the cattle he's buyin'. Sent his brother instead. Him I never knew. He must've come after I left the Box Double S."

He hadn't said anything about his relationship to Voni. Yet his tone had betrayed a deep interest.

"Yes," Marks replied. "They say someone put a bullet in Miss Voni's pa, in his back." He saw Smiley's mouth sag open with a painful gasp, his eyes grow wide. "He's laid up, but getting better. He'll pull out of it all right."

"You don't say." Smiley swung off his horse and stomped around to shake out the stiffness in his legs as well as the shock. He kept shaking his head, amazed. He was trembling, then angry.

"They find the man that did it?"

"No. They can't figure out anyone with that strong a reason. Matt Scovil is well-liked. He's done right by everyone. That's what they say."

"True, true. Well, if that don't beat all. Matt got gulched. But it's sweet news he's pullin' through. All iron an' rawhide that man is. Like Spellman. Like Bart Qualls, our ramrod here. An' Voni—is she lookin' good, as always?"

"Snatches your breath away." At that, Smiley chuckled. Marks warmed up to this man. If he was any judge of character, Smiley was cut out of the old rock, a man to have as a friend.

"Well, that's as always. Takes my breath away." A wistful look was etched deeply on the cowboy's face. Then he sighed, and his lips drew up to a kind of tightness.

"You talk like you know her kind of special," Marks ventured.

"You might say that." Smiley had swung back into his saddle. Now he gazed deliberately away toward the cutting work. But Marks observed from his neck muscles that he swallowed hard. And he lapsed into silence. Marks suspected what he confirmed as soon as Smiley turned his head back. Traces of moistness in his eyes gleamed like silver dewdrops on morning grass where sunbeams play. The cowboy shouldered a great sadness that made him reticent.

"Speaking of Miss Voni," said Marks as his eyes swept to the northeast, "there she rides. Coming out to watch 'em cut the last cattle."

Smiley came alive in his saddle. His eyes were grabbed as though by magnets to the girl on the clay-bank.

"Come on," said Marks, "let's ride with her." He sent his sorrel plunging down into the arroyo, spraying sand and clambering up the far bank. Smiley followed.

Voni drew rein and waited for the two riders. She recognized Marks who came first, far in the lead. But she was so intent on greeting him that she did not really take a good look at the second man.

"Howdy, Voni."

She seemed to jump, startled, and whirled to look. Her eyes widened and her pretty lips fell open.

"Smiley!" He sat in his saddle, a joyous grin wanting to play at the corners of his mouth but a hesitation in his eyes.

"Seems like a long, long time. Time has done you well. Yo're prettier than the most beautiful theater girls in Denver."

"Thank you." She smiled, then tightened into some reserve. "It has been a long time since—"

"Yeah, I know. Since I rode away." He cleared his throat, for emotion had made his voice labored, husky. "Voni, I'd have given anything . . ."

Marks was sure these two had treasured a very special friendship. The wounds of parting had not out-lasted tenderness, a feeling that went deep.

"Anything?" she replied, gazing off at a northern ridge beyond the Ponil. "Maybe 'anything' is too big a word for me to grasp, Smiley. What does it mean?"

Smiley seemed uneasy. He couldn't manage words. Voni gathered up her reins and stole a glance at him. But their eyes never met. Then she booted the claybank to a lope toward the herds. Smiley slumped, beaten, behind his saddlebow. He flung a despairing glance at Marks, felt a lump in his throat, and shrugged. Cut to the quick, he spun his horse resolutely.

3

Frank Spellman flung himself into the work as hard as any man in the outfit. He helped cut out longhorns Scovil agreed on.

One of the riders kept count by dropping pinto beans in two leather pouches. For every animal cut into the trail herd from Spellman's cattle, a bean went into one bag. For every critter separated from Griner's herd to make the trip north, a bean went into a smaller pouch.

Some of the "mossy horns" that loved the brush tangles were in a nasty mood. They were still riled that riders had pestered them out of their haunts and mastered them during the roundup. Now they stubbornly wanted to stay with the herd they were in and not be forced into a new bunch. Frequently one would make a headlong rush for the heavier brush. Riders and mounts had to be always wary of a belligerent steer's sudden charge. Those gouging horns, as deadly as a Green River knife blade, could spill and gut a mount. Then the danger loomed that a critter could gore a cowboy caught afoot.

Marks and Smiley worked the north side of the roundup herd Spellman had gathered. They cut out animals and drove them to the growing herd destined for

Colorado Territory. Spellman was working there, too. Hack Griner and two of his men cut steers from Griner's roundup bunch several hundred yards off to the north, bringing them to the trail herd.

Spellman cut out two steers to the edge of the herd and urged them east to add to the trail herd. Marks and Smiley had just turned from hazing a steer into the cut. A sudden movement snatched their attention. Two steers wheeled away to the south and made a furious tear for a brush-lipped wash that sliced out of the west.

Spellman's horse, a zebra dun color, raced down a gentle slant in hot pursuit. Suddenly the perverse bovines, as if carrying out a plot, veered in two directions. Spellman sent his eager horse fast on the heels of the one on his left. Marks spurred to head off the troublemaker on the right, and Smiley swept pell-mell after him to gang up on the steer. They heard the maddened bellow of the one Spellman chased as it crashed through tall, thick brush, plunged into the deep wash, and plowed sand surging for the bar bank. Spellman's dun made a flying leap from the lip of the wash into the sand four feet lower and a spray of sand shot upward. As the horse's front hooves hit the bottom of the wash, the saddle lurched forward with a pop. Suddenly, with its rider, it was pitched through space.

Above the pounding hoofbeats and crash of brush, a woman's terrified scream lifted on the air.

Marks hauled his own horse to a stop and threw a glance. He was just in time to see a bundle of man and saddle dropped from the air into the wash. The zebra dun, free of saddle and rider, scrambled on through loose sand behind the steer, which struck the far brush with a savage whack.

Marks wheeled his horse and sent him slapping over low brush to get to Spellman. Leaping his mount into the cushion of sand in the wash, he swung to the ground, digging in his heels to come to a stop. Spellman's body lay crumpled over a huge, gnarled chunk of driftwood that a spring flood had wrestled down. The rancher groaned, his face twisted in agony.

Smiley, too, turned back. He saw the steer Spellman had pursued lunge up the opposite bank and swing left. The animal dashed toward Voni, who had screamed when Spellman's saddle busted loose. She had dismounted on the far bank of the wash and had found a seat on a boulder about five feet up. From her perch she could watch the cutting work.

When Voni saw the bovine mass of destruction veer toward her, she slid down, scrambling to her claybank tied to a juniper a few yards away. She reached the horse and snatched up the reins. The steer's bellow was loud and bloodcurdling. The animal meant to blast a hole out of the world. Voni knew he was charging toward her, now not more than twenty feet away.

She grabbed the saddle horn and tried desperately to slam a boot into the stirrup. The claybank, squealing in panic, shot out of his tracks and jerked the stirrup away. The leap carried Voni with the horse, her fingers frozen to the horn in a wild clutch of strength. The steer rushed up, the tip of a horn catching the back of her blouse and ripping it from her back and shoulders.

The sideways bolt of the girl's horse had carried it to the bank of the wash. There the earth gave way beneath the weight, and the claybank spilled into the wash below. The girl, her grip wrenched from the horn, crashed astraddle of the brush fringing the bank, her head and shoulders hanging into the wash. The crazed steer whirled and came snorting back. Kicking her legs frantically to free herself from the tangle, Voni could not see the huge destroyer bearing down on her. She only heard the awesome snort and the pounding hooves coming back.

Smiley had seen. He drove spurs brutally to his horse. He swept at breakneck speed across the wash at an angle and streaked along the bank where Voni had been hurled. Gripping his saddle horn, he whipped his body down, caught the girl about her trim waist, and snatched her away. The steer's menacing face and horns reached the edge just as the girl's boots leaped up from the brush. Smiley bore the rescued girl on his strong arm, lifting her as he pulled himself upright. The horse surged on.

The steer slammed through the brush, carrying much of it with him. He lost his footing as he struck the wash, bellowed, then scrambled up and ascended the bank again to make a furious getaway.

Rounding a bend of the wash to safety, Smiley hauled his horse to a stop. He saw the steer tearing off in a different direction. Swinging down, the cowboy laid Voni on a carpet of thick grama grass in the shade of a tall juniper. Quickly he shucked his shirt to wrap about her.

"Here, this'll do," he said gently. He looked away, blushing slightly. She covered the petticoat with the shirt. "You all right, Voni?"

"Yes." She still trembled and her heart pounded like a drum. She sank down and put her face in her hands. Her head had been reeling, and her thoughts were only gradually clearing. Smiley's big hand, soft on her shoulder, felt reassuring. "Oh!" She suddenly remembered. "Mr. Spellman!"

Marks gently eased Spellman off of the twisted driftwood. He lowered him, using the sand as a cushion to lay him on.

"I'm busted up bad," the rancher groaned. He gritted his teeth against the racking pain. "Feels like every rib is broken. My leg . . . ahhhh-o-w-w-w!"

Hap Bailey pounded over at a gallop. He checked on his boss, who sprawled with his head in Marks's hands. Then he knelt beside the overturned saddle that had flopped into the wash. His mouth erupted in a disgusted growl. Then he held up part of the latigo strap.

"Cut . . . cut clean with a knife!" He shook his head for a long moment. "Had to be on purpose. Sliced in a V with just enough leather on each side of the slice to hold till Frank put some extra pressure on it. An' he was bound to do that." He slammed a clenched fist into the sand. His face, usually happy as his name implied, became heated with anger. "Some varmint plotted an accident."

Qualls, the ranch ramrod, swung off his horse. He knelt beside Spellman. Seeing his boss was alive, even able to talk, his big frame emitted an enormous sigh of relief. "How bad? Can you tell yet?" Marks replied that Spellman felt as if his ribs and leg were broken. Learning this, Qualls stood up and barked orders. "Hap, you know somethin' about doctorin'. Look after him till I can have a man fetch Doc from town. I'll tell him to run the legs off his horse. Marks, tell Jawbone to clear out a spot in the chuck wagon an' get it over here. We'll take Frank to the house. *Muy pronto!*"

As Marks scrambled to his horse, he heard the segundo say, "The lady's OK. Just shook up an' white as a sheet. Smiley's one hunk of a good man."

Marks lifted his mount to a hard run. His mind

41

reeled. How would Spellman fare? His guess was that this man Lonan highly respected would heal well, even if slowly. He was tougher than bull hide. But what would this injury do to the trail drive? Spellman would no doubt say go ahead on schedule. He might ride along in a ranch wagon or leave the bossing completely to Qualls. And from what Marks had heard among the men, Spellman couldn't find a finer trail boss in Texas or New Mexico Territory.

Qualls rode to the house that evening and had a palaver with Spellman at his bedside. Doc Tilden had ridden out from Cimarron to work on the rancher, but later had had to head on to another place where a boy was burning up with a high fever.

"Tally hit fifteen hundred," the ramrod reported. "We can move 'em out day after tomorrow, come sunup. Boys are dog-tired, but they ought to be rested by then. In the mornin', we'll get at it 'fore sunup, an' the men'll cut out the other five hundred. But while they're finishin' that, I want to look things over one last time over on the west range."

Marks stuck his head into the living room where they had set up Spellman's bed. "Mr. Spellman, I'd like to go with the herd. Pay or no pay. Do I have your OK? Lonan decided to go with Shaddo to Abilene, so I'm free."

Qualls had turned to leave. He hesitated, then came back. His voice was firm as flint but not unkind.

"We don't need a kid along, Frank. No time to do any nursemaidin'. We'll have plenty to keep us jumpin' as it is."

Spellman stared up at his ramrod and back at Marks's earnest face, pondering. In these past few weeks

Lonan had taught him a lot of respect for what the Dunlees were made of. Tough stuff like that would help the Southwest settle well against all odds. The Dunlees' pa, "Buckskin" Tom, had rescued Spellman from a Comanche death trap years before. Spellman was not able to imagine a Dunlee who couldn't take care of himself and then some.

"Awful good of you to offer." The rancher's voice was kind. He studied the frame that was already man-sized. "I savvy any son of Tom Dunlee has done a man's job from the time he was knee-high to a dogie. But it's risky. If the herd stampeded, or those Indians hit us, you could be hurt or . . . Well, I wouldn't want to tell a man that saved my life that I sent his boy to his death."

"Pa sent me on the drive we just finished," Marks said respectfully. "And I've been on other drives."

Lonan suddenly stood in the doorway.

"Speakin' in Pa's place as he's often let me do, I'll vouch for my brother. It's OK, Frank. The kid knows the angles. Has a lot of cow savvy. Already he's the best shot with a rifle in our family. If you run into Utes or Coe's gang, you could use that. An' if you need a man to read sign, Marks stacks up with the best. He's as good as Tom Tobin in Colorado, the man that tracked down the Espinosa killers. His age? No matter. It's what a man can do, not just whether he's thirty or seventeen. I'd take him on a drive like Shaddo did. Feel good to have him."

Marks swallowed hard, looked away, felt his eyes moist. Big words coming from an older brother he respected so much. Lonan had taught him many things that make a man a man. So had Shaddo and Shiloh and most of all Pa.

Thoughts flashed back to a cabin hidden in a grove

43

of cottonwoods and willows in the Texas panhandle, not far from the Red River. Lonan and Marks had come across their Uncle Jack lying facedown on the trail, dying in his own blood. The two robbers of their mother, whom Uncle Jack had pursued, had laid in wait for him. Later, Lonan and Marks saw the cabin, and found one of the murderers gasping his final words on the hard dirt floor. The other outlaw had shot him to get all of the robbery money and had fled to the Arkansas River to go to Colorado Territory. Lonan had looked at Marks.

"One of us needs to take Uncle Jack back, kid. One has to stay on the trail. You get along home, boy. I'll follow the killer."

So the older, more experienced Dunlee clung to the trail of the robber and killer. Now he was talking as if his young brother had grown some.

"I meant no offense," Qualls said softly. "But I never saw a kid that young do all of that. An' I don't like to see a kid get hurt before he's lived half his years. He'll be some man, but right now . . ."

"Why don't we think on it a spell," suggested Spellman. He gritted his teeth in pain. "Now, men, let me get some rest. Bart, I don't know if you've had time to give it any thought yet, but I'd stake a guard. One here an' one to nose around the cattle camp. We don't want any more latigo straps cut."

A couple hours after sunup Marks spotted Qualls riding out from the ranch.

"He's headin' out to make a final check on some range and stock he left out of the roundup," Smiley said.

"I'd like to get on better terms with him," Marks said. "Catch him alone. Maybe we can talk it out. Anyhow, I need a ride." He laid a blanket on the sorrel and threw on the saddle. "I hope things look better between you and Miss Voni."

"Uh, she's nice to me, but I can't figure it out for sure," Smiley replied. "Every time I've tried to get close to talk, 'Saber-tooth,' the gunslinger, hovers like a shadow. Scovil pays him to be bodyguard for him an' Voni. Me, I reckon Tontam's overplayin' it. It's like Tontam's afraid she'll say somethin' he doesn't want her to. Or some other gent will be friendly with her."

Marks nodded and settled into his saddle. "Your chance may come. If not here, at the end of the drive. She looks like she'd be some lady to go after. But looks don't tell the whole story, you know." He rode off, waving to Jackie who had appeared in the doorway.

Not more than fifteen minutes behind Qualls, he followed the tracks of his horse off to the west. The trail of bent grass and hoofprints led toward the Sangre de Cristo. The peaks loomed in rugged blue majesty.

An hour later, Marks scanned the range from a low hill. He caught sight of the foreman circling a mud hole, no doubt glad to find no critter bogged. The ramrod struck a cow path into high brush and vanished from view. But beyond the brush Marks could see a pasture of yellowed grama touched by a scattering of green juniper clumps. And past it was a broad strip of low bench land garbed with stands of piñons, junipers, and a variety of brush.

He pushed his field glasses firmly back into a saddle-bag and jogged on. Once inside the thicket, he came to a sign that made him draw up. He noticed fresh horse tracks coming in from the north via another cow trail through the brush. As he followed, he noticed that the prints were on top of those Qualls's mount had left. The second horseman was following Qualls!

Once at the far side of the tall brush, Marks peered through the glasses again. Over at the far left end of the pasture, a cow emerged from a mot of trees. She was moving faster than necessary, as if frightened from her place. Marks combed the area patiently with the glasses, shading them with his hat so as not to let the sunlight reflect on them and give his presence away. All of a sudden he saw a man's hat and shoulders between limbs of trees. The man, obviously atop a horse, could gaze over a lower area beyond. Probably he could watch Qualls working his way toward the bench.

The mysterious rider appeared to be stalking. Then he was gone.

A few minutes later, after riding a cautious loop around the left end of the pasture to remain out of sight, Marks picked up the rider's tracks. The hoofprints swung in a thin half-circle to intercept Qualls if he clung to a rather straight course. What was the man up to?

A bit farther on, Marks swung up to the crest of a small knoll. He gasped. A man stood about a hundred yards to his right in a deep ravine beneath a cottonwood. Qualls was riding toward this spot but about a hundred horse strides away, unaware. The thing that really grabbed Marks's attention was the rifle the man held. It was trained on Qualls!

Marks ducked back and eased his sorrel out of sight. He was careful not to give away his presence by a sound. Moving stealthily as an Indian, he worked around behind the ambusher afoot and scurried to a spot half-hidden behind a slab of rock. Pointing his .44, he waited. Qualls, who had dismounted at the command of the ambusher, spotted Marks, blinked, but covered his surprise. The ramrod's holster was empty, so the ambusher must have forced him to throw down his pistol.

"What do you aim to do with me?" Qualls demanded.

"Easy question. Take you down one of these draws where the sound won't carry. I'll cover you with dirt from the bank." The plotting killer motioned with his rifle. "Might as well say yore last prayers."

"No need," Qualls drawled. "I've been on the best o' terms with the God I say 'em to." He wet his lower lip deliberately, letting his words register. "Besides, I aim to be around after they have you in jail."

The man scoffed. The rifle pointed at the foreman's heart and the hand was steady. Nothing could throw him off now.

"Throw down the gun or you're dead!" Marks barked the words loaded with authority. The ambusher's chin dropped and his entire frame went rigid as if quick-frozen. For one brief moment he weighed his chances. Then he wagered they were very slim. He could not whirl, spot his target, and hit it before a slug tore him apart. His fingers relaxed on the rifle. He bent, his arm extended outward, and let the weapon drop safely into dried leaves.

Qualls was quick to grab up his own weapon. He stared at Marks as if at a delivering angel. A revelation had passed before his vision, and it held him powerfully. The two men ordered the ambusher to fall on his stomach, and the ramrod bound rawhide cords about his wrists behind his back.

"His horse is close by," Qualls said. "Fetch it."

Marks went into the brush where a light bay waited hipshot. He led the bay to Qualls, and they prodded the man aboard. Marks brought his sorrel and dropped the loop of his riata around the would-be killer's neck.

"Just so you don't get any crazy notion about making a run for it," he said. He handled the rope in his free hand as he took up his reins. Qualls's face wrinkled in a knowing, pleased ghost of a smile. He raked up his own reins and stepped astride his horse.

"Let's head on back," the foreman said. Taking the reins of the captive's animal, he led the way he had come. Marks brought up the rear. As they crossed the pasture traversed a few minutes earlier, Qualls twisted in his saddle and threw a measuring glance on Marks. "You handle things top-notch, kid. I dunno why you trailed me, but if you hadn't, I'd have sand caved in my face. I owe you my life." He rode on a ways. Then he turned again. "So, you hanker to go on the drive?" He broke into a broad grin. "I say fine. Yo're one man I want. By the way, why did you tail me?"

"Just figured I'd jaw with you," replied the younger rider, grinning broadly. "No need now. It's all taken care of."

They were within four miles of the layout when Marks's sorrel tossed his head off to the right and snorted, nostrils flaring. The first thing that seized the young horseman's mind was that they were in a bad place. Out in an open stretch, they had no defense against an attack. And Utes and Apaches prowled the land.

A bullet hummed across the flatland. Marks heard the crack of a rifle. Death seemed to be a part of the bullet's whine.

4

The sullen captive, who rode in a slouchy slump, jerked sideways as though hammered by a powerful blow. The two who rode with him heard a desperate, choking cry. A couple more shots twanged off in a high thicket. The prisoner tumbled from his horse, his left boot hanging in the stirrup.

Marks glimpsed wisps of smoke a hundred paces away. He had shucked his Winchester. Though jerked about by the sorrel's startled prancing, he snapped off a pair of shots into the tangle. Stepping clear of the saddle on the side away from the bushwhacker, he took the rope dally off the horn with a quick hand. That let the falling man have all the slack. Out of a corner of an eye he knew Qualls also had gone off his horse to the protected side. The segundo sent a bullet over the distance, then another.

No more rifle reply came from the concealment. Glances at the bushwhacker's target gave both riders an instant message. This had been the man's last ride. His last day of living had been a sorry one.

Marks leaped back on his mount and reined him off to the northeast. He swung in an arc toward the killer's nest. As he rode, he hung low on the front shoulder of his pounding horse, affording no target if the rifleman lingered. The sorrel whipped through low brush to the left of the gulcher's lurking place, and Marks brought him to a grinding stop.

The moment the sorrel's hoofbeats were still, Marks heard the thud of another horse off to the southeast. A man small in the distance was flung low over the mane of a gray roan and beating his horse to get away.

"Yonder," Marks yelled to Qualls, who was spurring to join him. The foreman only momentarily slowed, then dug spurs and streaked past.

"Let's get 'im!"

The pursued had only a quarter-mile head start. But he picked ravines and brush well and was on a fast horse. Soon he lengthened his advantage as they swept over the miles to the southeast. After a few miles, Qualls yelled above the drone of hooves.

"He's headin' right to a place where he could stop a detachment from Fort Union." Marks knew from his rough map that the fort was some miles to the south, past Cimarron and Rayado.

Qualls jerked a big hand toward a rugged ridge a mile away and pulled his horse to a stop. "We'd ride right into a burst of his gunfire, an' he could pick us off easy." He drew a hand across a sweating brow and shook his head ruefully. He hated to give up the prey. "He could find a dozen places to hole up, where he could riddle a whole cavalry outfit. No, boy, he's not lurin' us up there. Suicide! That wouldn't do Frank any good. He needs us."

He wheeled his horse, and Marks grasped the wisdom of his judgment. He fell in with the ramrod. There were people he'd like to go back to—alive. People such as

Pa and Ma, his brothers, his sister Becky, and people like the Spellmans.

He and Qualls saved their own lives and rode back to pick up the dead man. When they rode into the ranch yard leading the horse with the man drooping from the saddle, the place came alive.

Spellman had been toted out to the yard on a bunk. He wanted to be able to see the barn, corrals, bunkhouse, and the range beyond. Now he gazed from fever-heated eyes as the riders drew up by the bunkhouse steps.

Jeanie came out beside her husband. She wore a pink apron with white flowers she had sewn into it, over a gingham dress. She laid a gentle hand on Frank's shoulder.

Scovil, for once without Tontam as his shadow, craned his neck with interest from his perch on a bench outside the cabin. He had been paging through a copy of the *Rocky Mountain News* that a stage had brought from Denver. Tontam had gone off to Cimarron.

A couple of ranch hands, black cowboy Smoky Dobis and huge Wile Gaster, showed at the bunkhouse door. They rubbed eyes bleary from the few hours of sleep they had had since riding night herd duty. Lonan and Shaddo, talking out by the corrals, strode over.

Marks saw Jackie walking up from Ponil Creek. She carried a bouquet, no doubt to decorate the supper table. When she saw the body slung over the horse, she gasped and drew the back of a hand over her mouth. Then Marks waved and she recognized him. She came on toward the house.

Wile Gaster turned the man's face to have a careful look. Neither he nor Smoky could identify the corpse.

"All I know is, he looks like a feller I saw hangin'

around Swink's bar in town a few days ago," Wile offered. "They was three of 'em, no, four, an' salty-lookin' hombres."

"Yessuh, sho was," Smoky recalled. "One was a big blond, like you, Wile, but not as big. Built like a butte. Had teeth like fangs on a wolf, an' mean eyes." He pondered and also remembered, "Nothah was squat, dark-bearded. Best ah remembahs, da third one was tall, dark, an' had a hook nose like a hawk."

"You never laid eyes on 'em before?" Qualls queried.

"Nope," said Wile. "They'd jest drifted in. I wondahed if they might be some of that gang William Coe jest started up in the Ratons, lookin' things ovah heah."

Gaster had ridden with outlaws himself till recently. He knew the breed.

Lonan turned the face and studied it. "I reckon," he said after some thought, "this here's Ike Klugger. Long way from his usual stompin' ground over around the Fort Worth country an' south. Suspected of rustlin'. Lucky he didn't get his neck stretched from a tall limb back there."

"Today," said Marks grimly, "he was nailed just as sure."

"Yeah, after Marks here caught 'im dead to rights," Qualls threw in. "Dead to rights—later dead."

Eyes turned to the youthful rider. "Marks killed 'im?" Lonan asked.

"No, wasn't me," Marks quickly denied. "I threw down on 'im when he was fixin' to do Mr. Qualls in. We were bringin' 'im in. Someone murdered 'im from the brush."

"We chased the killer a ways," the ramrod took it

up. "He was movin' like a wolf jest ahead of a timber fire. So we turned back."

"What is it?" Jeanie called from the bedside near the house.

Qualls dismounted, shook his legs at the saddle weariness, and handed the reins to Wile. Then he strode with a jingle of spurs to fill the Spellmans in on the incident. Later he rejoined the knot of men by the bunkhouse.

"Marks, I've got to ask a favor," he said. "Someone's got to take the body in to the sheriff. He'll want to talk to one of us. I've got too much to do 'fore we pull out. I'd like you to take care o' this. Wile, you an' Smoky ride along. Three o' you oughta be safe if you run into those hombres."

He told Wile and Smoky to get back in time to catch some sleep before reporting for early morning duty at the herd.

Marks tied the killer's horse to a cottonwood at the corner of the bunkhouse and hastily saddled a fresh mount. Then he walked over to speak to the Spellmans before Wile and Hank got their gear on their horses.

After a brief word with Spellman and his wife, he saw Jackie inside the doorway. She smiled.

"Marks, you need some coffee before you go," the girl said. So he walked into the house, and she poured him a cup.

"I'm so glad it wasn't one of our men," she exclaimed with feeling. "Only a short time ago we received the word . . . that is, we thought my pa had been killed. Your brother Lonan found out he was still alive, being held captive. Now, every time I think of a death, I shudder."

He savored a swallow of the coffee. "So do I. Let's hope we never get over that. Life's a gift, and I want to hold on to it as long as I can." She nodded agreement, and he glanced at a gallery of daguerreotypes and paintings set up on a dresser in the living room.

"This is Pa a few years ago," she pointed out. "This is Ma. And this painting is Pa and Ma in their wedding clothes." He could tell how proud Jackie was from the beam in her eyes. His gaze moved on and was held by a daguerreotype of a small girl. She was perhaps seven or eight.

"Oh, this one I treasure too!" Jackie said with enthusiasm. "A family in Virginia visited in Kentucky. I met the two sisters, Teresa and Mandie. I love Mandie so much! This is her when she was younger than the time when I met her. The only picture I have. A rancher near here, Shoat Hartman, gave it to me. When he rode over to visit Pa, he said he had a daughter in Virginia named Mandie. What a coincidence. She was the same girl. When he saw how much I loved Mandie, he said he'd bring me a picture. He had two copies. Sure enough, a few days later one of his men, Luke Savage, brought this.

"I do hope Mr. Hartman will someday see Mandie again. And I want to as well."

Marks picked up the picture, set in a polished wooden frame. He liked the bright eyes, the well-formed mouth, and the happiness that seemed to glow in the cheeks. Her hair tumbled down to her shoulders, and she wore a ribbon in her hair.

Jackie stared at the Texas rider. "Why, Marks. What is it about this picture? You don't even know Mandie."

He looked sheepish, fumbled for words. "She reminds me of someone—my sister, Becky. We were always close."

"You really love Becky. I can tell."

"Yeah. I think Becky's . . . well, when I was real young I told her I wanted to marry her when it comes time. Kid stuff, you know. Ma heard that. She said I couldn't marry Becky."

"And what did *you* say?" she teased.

"Well, what do you say? I jest said, 'Then I'll find someone *like* Becky.' "

She laughed. Then she described Mandie. He listened, shaking his head approvingly. "Yeah, that's Becky all over. Strange thing is, she looks so much like Becky. I mean, the eyes are sort of laughing, daring. And the corners of the mouth."

"You'd like Mandie." She was gazing off in the distance. "She isn't a little girl anymore. She's a girl going into her teens. And prettier than this. Such a lovely person! God never made one better."

"Hey, Marks. We're all set." It was Wile Gaster's booming voice from out by the bunkhouse. Marks's mind was snatched back to the task at hand. He set down the framed copper plate very carefully.

Reaching the door, he turned back. "Good coffee. Good pictures." Then he waved and stepped out to get to his horse.

"Yes, Marks." Jackie picked up the last picture again and stood laughing about past moments she'd enjoyed with Mandie. "Good pictures, but especially one."

Then she heard the thud of horses' hooves leaving the yard.

Riding with the others, Marks was quiet for a long

time. A gentle sweetness seemed to ride with him. He did not want to let it go.

After the riders left for Cimarron, Scovil came over from the bunkhouse. He, too, had looked at the body. He'd been listening to conjectures about the ambush attempt. Now he lit up a perfecto. He thrust his fingers under his belt and shook his head in amazement.

"Any idea, Frank, why all these things are happenin'? Who could be back of it? What would be the reason?"

"Yeah, I've got some idea," Spellman growled. His face contorted in discomfort. "I keep thinkin' someone doesn't want me along on the drive. Now this Ike shows up an' tries to take out my trail boss. Qualls is the best. Losin' him could've really weakened us for the drive."

"But why?" Scovil pressed. "Why would anyone hit you *before* a drive?"

"Well," said Frank, "that dead man ran with outlaws, rustlers, I think. Lonan recognized 'im. The timin' o' this, right before the drive, suggests that someone wants our trail crew to be weaker. I suspect they want to take advantage along the trail north."

"Hanged if they will!" Scovil exploded. He agitated the perfecto nervously, and banged a fist against a stone of the cabin. "We can't let anybody get the herd. My brother needs those cattle. Needs 'em bad. I swore he'd have 'em. An' he said he could count on you gettin' the cattle to him."

"Put it down. He *can* count on it," Spellman said with feeling. "We've got the outfit. If rustlers plot what we think, they're losers so far. True, they've got me down, but I'll be back. One of their men is dead, an' he won't come back. Now we're forewarned. We'll be ready for anything."

"How do you figger? Will there be any trouble *here* after the men leave with the herd?" Scovil puffed at his perfecto. "Or will the rustlers just be after the herd?"

"Oh, I figger the herd. They'll wait till the herd's a long way from here. Here it's too risky. We've got too many friends close by—Lucien Maxwell, Sheriff Stover, Shoat Hartman, an' more. Besides, I'm keepin' a couple o' men. Not only that, but Hack Griner promised me two men from his outfit!"

"Good, then," Scovil said in relief. "My brother an' I need this herd. But we don't want *you* to be in any danger."

He dismissed himself to talk with Voni, who was in her bedroom. Spellman lay staring at the corrals, wondering why Scovil spent so much time checking on Voni.

5

A small crowd gathered quickly when the three dismounted at the hitching rail by the sheriff's office. A boy running ahead had alerted the lawman, who tromped out.

"This heah's Sheriff Stover," Wile Gaster said. "Meet Marks Dunlee, from Texas."

"Know Lonan Dunlee," said the sheriff. "I set store by him. Heared you Dunlee fellers was with an outfit bringin' cattle for Frank. Now, who's the body? How'd it happen?"

"Name's Ike Klugger," Marks replied. "Rode the outlaw trail. We caught him tryin' to gun down Bart Qualls. When we were totin' him to the Spellman place, a bushwacker knocked him off his horse. He was dead when he landed."

Gaster spoke up. "He was with three othahs Smoky Dobis heah an' I saw comin' outta Swink's bar a few days back."

Marks glimpsed Lacy Tontam standing in the crowd. Tontam's grulla stood slack-hipped at the hitching rail in front of Lucien Maxwell's trading post. Someone had said that Tontam had ridden to town to send a letter by the stage line that ran into Colorado Territory.

"Let's tote him inside," said the sheriff. "You can fill me in on the whole story."

Tontam licked his lips thoughtfully. Then he spun around and strode straight to his grulla. Drawing up the slack in the cinch strap, he stepped into the saddle and booted the horse to a lope northward over the bridge of Cimarron Creek and out of town. Three miles to the northeast, he looked backward and forward to make sure nobody was coming. Then he cut away on rocky ground, careful to leave no tracks. He dropped down into a deep wash and stuck with its snakelike twists northwest.

Three men hunkered by a small fire, sipping hot coffee out of tin cups. The smoke lifted lazily, thinned, and vanished in the overhanging limbs of a cottonwood. Nearby, three horses chomped at grama grass. One mount, a gray roan, was lathered from a punishing run.

"Yeah, I'm shore," a squat man with a darkly bearded face emphasized. He answered to the name Donk Bodeen. "I saw 'em turn back, then spotted 'em a couple miles away. They wasn't about to face in toward the ridge. I could pick 'em off. Once they gave it up, I circled back."

"Good!" The tall blond with sharp buck teeth was pleased. Fang Gatril raked a dirty mop of yellow hair back from wolf green eyes and stared at his half-emptied cup. "They'll blame it on Coe's Robbers' Roost gang."

"When do we pull out for Trinidad an' north?" asked Jack Mangis, whom they called "Hawk." He was tall, lean, hook-nosed, and had a furtive, hungry look. His face was matted with dirty black hair. "I wanta pick up the rest o' the men. Hacker won heavy off'n me, an' I aim to win it back."

"Ah, quit fidgetin'," the blond growled. "You'll get yore chance quick enough. Hacker's probly let it run through his fingers by now anyhow. He's at Trinidad, with whiskey, cards, an' women. We ain't in ary hurry. Now the attention's on Coe. We're free an' clear. So we bide our time. Me, I don't crave havin' to push hard nohow, always havin' to get away from someone. We'll go easy till we hit the herd. I'm tired o' runnin'."

"Hey, I hear somethin'!" Bodeen hissed a warning. He sprang up fast as a cougar. Grabbing his rifle, he hustled to a bend in the wash to squint through overhanging brush. "Rider comin'," he grunted.

The other two hastily slapped blankets and saddles on their horses and cinched up. Mangis tossed a blanket on Bodeen's lathered roan.

"It's all right," Bodeen finally informed them. "Jest the fast 'un payin' us a visit."

"Tontam!" The blond breathed easier and pulled his saddle off. Then he retrieved his cup from the grassy bank where he'd tossed it down in haste. Sloshing more coffee into the cup, he gulped the contents down and stalked out to throw up his huge arm in greeting.

Tontam brought his grulla in at a walk. Halting a few feet from Gatril, he sat sweeping the camp scene with contempt. He himself had lived better than this on the trail.

"Not very cozy," he drawled. Criticism sharpened the words to cut at those who were touchy. He had never hit it off well with Gatril, so it was a carnal pleasure to take a dig at the man skulking in discomfort. "You ain't gonna savor the news I've got."

"The devil you say." Gatril was a tense animal, dark suspicion slinking into his cruel eyes. "What is it? Out with it!"

"Seems like they recognized Ike," Tontam said as he let the impact sink in. "Yeah, tied 'im in with you boys, not William Coe's gang over at Black Mesa. Some o' the Spellman roundup crew showed up in Cimarron. Had Ike slung over his horse. They was speakin' o' him by name. Some of 'em had seen him with you three at Swink's saloon. So they know yo're here, hangin' 'round Cimarron."

The hairy-faced Bodeen exploded in a loud, snarling curse. He stomped a boot heel violently at the sand, pawing dust like a maddened bull.

"Seen us at Swink's." Mangis mumbled it out of a contortion of pain. Understanding showed in eyes that were deep caves in his dark face. "Yeah, someone said men o' the FS brand was in town."

"One thing's a cinch," Tontam said, as if twisting a blade in them. "Won't take that tin star Stover long to run through his wanted notices. Once he sees yore faces for murder, horse thievin', an' rustlin', he might figger Captain Coe's outfit didn't have ary hand in things here. Stover's straight as a gun barrel. An' he'll ransack the country to flush you."

The impact of the obvious sank to the quick in Gatril. He swallowed hard and took up the angry spewing against the rotten luck. His sidekicks were still muttering. Finally Gatril delivered himself of the expletives in his limited vocabulary.

"All right, all right." He resigned himself darkly. "So we run again." He scowled wickedly, then turned on the mounted gunman. "Obliged for the tip. But why does it have to be delivered with a smirk? You, the fair-haired boy, ridin' with the boss, the big auger, fillin' yore eyes all day with the purty lady, sleepin' in fine beds, slurpin' the best o' food, keepin' yore hands clean. An' we do the dirty work, live in the brush like wild turkeys, live on a hair-trigger."

"Aw, quit the bellyachin'," Tontam said. "You made yore own bed. You bought yore ticket. You were willin' to take risks for the big slices you'll get. Me, I take risks too."

"Risks? You an' the big man have this down so smooth you come out shinin'. It's cussed little risk left for you. Anyhow, I don't like that taunt you put in yore voice, like you was laughin' inside at us havin' to git. Cut the smirk or one of these days I'll smear it back on yore face."

Tontam cackled as he looked down on the other man. His free right hand was poised at a familiar place casually on his thigh. Fingers clenched and unclenched to limber them, as a rattler coils before it strikes. A generous heaping of contempt rode his cackle.

"No time like the present," he suggested. "Yore gun is closer to yore hand than mine is. Why don't you try it?"

"Aw, you two bulls quit yer pawin' the dust," Bodeen snapped. He stepped between them. "Tontam, you done us a favor. You warned us. Now we light a shuck outta here. If we fight among ourselves, someone ain't gonna get no payoff money."

Gatril raked the back of a grimy hand across his mouth. He shrugged and turned to gather a few items into his bedroll. He wanted dearly to get at Tontam—get at his jugular with bare hands, not with a gun. He liked the surer way.

The corners of Tontam's mouth peeled back in pleasure. He knew Gatril was relieved to have the excuse to turn away. He watched the three men paw sand to hide their campfire and hastily break camp. Then he gathered up his reins and jerked the grulla about.

"We'll be in touch with yore messenger at the cabin near Trinidad," he called back. Then he spurred to a lope across the wash, slashing east to return to the FS ranch house.

Smoky and Wile went to Swink's and later to the Lucien Maxwell mansion to ask about the three strangers. The sheriff and Marks strode over to the stables that Maxwell kept. There they talked with the hostler.

"Yeah," he said. "They was four of 'em here this mornin'. They rode out to the west. Hard-bitten bunch. They could bite an axle in two. Hardly said a word. Jest mean-lookin'. Me, I figger they're watchin' over their shoulders."

"Hang it all," said Sheriff Stover, "if I'd o' looked through them wanted notices agin the last three, four days I might've recognized 'em."

"They may be campin' close," Marks suggested. "The one we chased could've swung around when we dropped off, an' headed for a rendezvous. We'll know if we can pick up their tracks an' follow 'em."

"Shore," the lawman replied. "First, let me go have a talk with Maxwell. I won't be more'n a half hour."

While waiting, Marks went to the Maxwell trading

post and bought a couple of new shirts, an extra pair of denims, some underwear, a new slicker, several boxes of .44 cartridges that would fit either his rifle or his Colt revolver, a new razor, hand soap, and a needle and thread.

This done, he set out to find a gift for Mrs. Spellman and Jackie. A music box seemed just the thing. So he had it wrapped, then rolled it up with other things inside his slicker tied behind the cantle.

The four men met at the stable. They were giving the horses a final drink before the ride when they heard a shout down at Doc Tilden's house.

"Looks like Katie Sutter," the lawman said. "Ma Sutter's been due. This must be her time."

They started to rein away to the west, but heard another shout. Katie rode hard to stop them. She was, Marks judged, about fifteen, a slender girl with an attractive freckled face.

"Sheriff!" she called urgently. She drew up her foam-flecked buckskin in a boil of dust. "I thought you'd better know. Ma's time has come. I was ridin' to fetch Doc. A man cut into the trail to block my way. Then I saw two others sneakin' up from the sides to box me in. They started laughin' an' sayin' ugly things. So I whirled Bucky here, an' broke clear when one of their horses stumbled. I cut through between two of 'em an' lit out. They came after me, but Bucky's awful fast, an' they gave it up."

"Ah, Katie, that's a sad thing to happen to you," said the sheriff. "What'd they look like?"

The girl's description brought a grunt from the sheriff and nods from Marks and the two FS riders.

"We'll ride back with you," Stover told Katie. "Doc'll come on behind. We're lookin' for them three.

Girl, you need a fresh horse." He yelled to the hostler, who was saddling Doc's horse. In a jiffy, the hostler had a horse ready for Katie.

About four miles east, Katie pointed out the place where the three men had tried to trap her. Riding a circle, Marks found trail signs of the three striking off to the northeast. So the tracking party decided that Smoky would accompany Katie and Doc on to the Sutter place, then head north and meet them at a point along Ponil Creek.

An hour later, far to the northeast, the lawman and his companions paused.

"They're movin' fast," Marks said as he interpreted the spacing and depth of the horse tracks. "They're pointin' to the Clifton House, or plan to rest the night at Uncle Dick Wootton's place the other side of Raton Pass. Or maybe, they'll try to make it all the way to Trinidad." He was recalling his study of Spellman's map.

"Another twenty-five miles to the Clifton House, forty-five to Trinidad," the bearer of the star said ruefully. He dug out a watch. "Half past five. You fellers could never ride that far an' get back for your night shift at the herd."

"An' we'd never leave you to go it alone," Marks rejoined. He stripped off his gear to give his horse a brief rubdown while they decided what to do. He rubbed the horse briskly with handfulls of grama grass he patiently gathered up.

"Yo're a good man with a horse," Stover observed. He followed suit, as did Wile Gaster. They had hardly gotten the gear off when Smoky emerged from an arroyo to the south, rejoining them.

"Helps a horse feel better," said Marks. "Still a long

66

ride ahead whether we go on or head back."

"Let's head on back," decided Stover. "I'll send word on to Trinidad by tomorrow mornin's stage. If the sheriff there spots 'em, I can ride over with men to give him a hand."

The chair with a cushion was a welcome seat after the wearying hours in the saddle. Thick steak, biscuits and gravy, and salad from Jeanie's garden were a treat. The ladies had kept the food warm.

Halfway through the meal, Marks took out the gift from his slicker. "Before leavin', I wanted to give you something you can remember me by. Just remember that when I gave it, it was for two people who made me feel the way I feel at home with Ma and my sister Becky."

The two ladies' cheeks flushed as the soft glow of the lamp played on the beauty of their faces. Many a day across the far reaches of sunswept loneliness he would cherish that picture. It would bring back a smiling tenderness against the toughening callous of the cattle trail.

Jeanie's fingers nimbly broke the seals of the brown paper wrapping. She laughed in girlish joy. This enlivened Marks like a tonic.

"Marks Dunlee, you and your talk of music!" She held the music box toward Jackie, and both ladies admired it. Jeanie let it play, and sat revelling.

"We'll cherish it." Jackie smiled. "It'll be special. When we play it, often, we'll say a special prayer that you'll be safe. Do you think that will help?"

"Prayer help? O, I do! I *know* it will. God does answer our prayers when we trust him!"

"The drive means something extra to me," Jeanie said. "Frank and I want it to help Josh and Jackie get a start. Then there's a second reason. All the men going mean very much to me, to us. Then there's you."

"Yes, there's me," Marks grinned. "I'm glad I count too."

"How did you ever guess?" Jeanie teased. "We have a favored place for you. Lonan has done so much for us, things we never could repay. We feel very close to your family. When the drive is underway, Jawbone will break out a surprise for all of the men. But here is a surprise for you—just you." She handed him a burlap sack, drawn up and bound tightly with cowhide thong. The contents were about half the size of his hat crown. "Sometime when you are alone, beyond the Ratons, open this. But no fair peeking ahead of time."

When Marks lay on his bunk later, he wondered what dangers the drive held in store. Indians, who had hit in various places since some had fled from Chivington's cavalry at the Sand Creek massacre in 1864, were an ever-present threat. Folk never knew when or where they might make a strike. Then there were lurking white outlaws; the blast of thirst if good water was not to be had; the peril of hunger-driven wolves; the suffering from a cold wind or early fall snow; the surging of a stampede; or a horse rolling over its rider. All of these Marks had already faced or seen.

He drifted off to sleep, touched by the gentle thought of a girl—a girl who affected him like no girl ever had, a lovely girl with flowing hair, a girl he had never met, a girl in a picture.

6

They moved the longhorns out by sunup. Two thousand critters started on the long trek north. Those Hu Scovil had chosen from the herd that came up the Pecos were not sleek and sassy like the steers added from Spellman's and Griner's home stock. But all would be travel-worn, sore of hoof, and perhaps more gaunt when they got to Matt Scovil's place beyond the Arkansas. Judging by reports on Scovil's grass, however, all would fatten quickly.

Eleven men made up the trail outfit. Joe "Jawbone" Daniels, the cook, handled the team pulling the chuck wagon. Bart Qualls, the boss or segundo (second to Spellman), rode ahead to scout country the longhorns would cross. As they started, Hap Bailey and Smiley Landon rode point. Chip Morrow and Pete Tallam rode on one side of the winding herd, while Wile Gaster and Smoky Dobis were on the other side. Shag Wootten and Marks Dunlee brought up the drag, and Todd Reardon handled the remuda.

Loop Sorrels and Tack Laycox stayed at the ranch to handle chores and protect the place. Two riders from

Hack Griner's spread were due over in a few days.

Qualls led the drive to the Red River or Canadian, which they reached the second morning out. Crossing the river before grazing them, they camped not far from Tom Stockton's new Clifton House, a tall trail hotel and stage stop. Stockton had come from Tennessee to Texas and on to New Mexico Territory. First he'd built a one-room cabin; now he was well along in building the big house over and around the initial one.

That afternoon they watered the herd at Willow Springs on the slope six miles up from the Clifton House. Smith Sayers lived there with his wife Sara Frances and four children in a two-room jacal on the west bank of the creek coming out of Willow Arroyo. He was building a four-room log cabin after coming in 1866, planning to stay.

"You'll pay to pass Wootton's, but here you're lucky," Sayers told Qualls as the riders watered the cattle. "Water here's free now, but I plan to sell it . . . maybe twenty-five cents a bucket."

"Man, you'll make money," the trail boss agreed. "You get a lot of traffic. Goodnight's been through with his herd not long ago, an' comin' with another. Must also be a lot of gold-seekers headed for the new bonanza, E-Town, an' quite a lot of stage traffic."

"Been a flock of folk," Sayers admitted. "For years. Back in 1846, I hear, General Stephen Kearney's soldiers and Colonel Alexander Donaphan's troops camped around the springs. Then they went south and claimed the territory from Mexico. 'Course, the government's had a forage station here for Fort Union soldiers since 1860."

Qualls glanced at the corrals and army warehouse not far away.

"Some day," he said, "it seems like a nice area for a town."

The drive went on up into Raton Pass, through deep gorges with massive mountains all around. In one stretch, the riders looked off to the east at flat-topped Fisher's Peak which loomed like a rock fortress. By noon the third day they descended to Uncle Dick Wootton's hotel house and his heavy cottonwood tollgate.

Wootton, one of the early settlers of Colorado Territory, had lived at Taos, Denver City, and Fountain Creek near Pueblo. Around 1865 he'd secured the right from the Colorado and New Mexico governments to improve a twenty-seven-mile strip of the Santa Fe Trail's mountain branch. The treacherous trail, boulder-strewn, wound above precipices and had been a wrecking place for wagons. Wootton's improved road ran from Trinidad on the Purgatoire River to the Clifton House by the Red River.

Qualls paid the toll for the cattle and horsemen plus the remuda. Wootton, a grizzled mountain man, dropped the money into a keg. The ramrod chafed at the necessity of such a toll, as Charley Goodnight had done not long before.

Only Indians, who would not think of paying to pass through land they felt was their own, and military men or lawmen got past Wootton's gate gratis.

The crew pushed on down the slope into Colorado Territory. Qualls called Marks to ride ahead with him to find a bedding ground with good grazing before dark.

"I like your work," the ramrod told Marks straight-out. "I set store by your brother Lonan. He said yo're a top hand findin' water an' grazin'. From here on, you scout ahead with me. We'll ride out a couple hours ahead of the herd in the mornin's."

"Sounds good." Marks grinned. "Word is you know this strip to the north, though."

"Yeah. I know some creeks that'll have water from recent rain. I expect to find grass, too. But we'll both need eyes in the backs of our heads to watch for Utes and Apaches. They've hit the Trinidad area a number of times, run off stock, an' killed folk. Captain Coe's gang is bad too. Besides, we've got to keep our eyes open for the killers Ike Klugger ran with."

"Both kinds, Indians on the prod or white scum, can be hard to deal with," Marks replied. "Shaddo and I had a short brush with Comanches near the Pecos. Just up from Horsehead Crossing. We'd scouted a good piece ahead of the herd when they pounced on us out of a draw."

"What happened?"

"Killed us both," Marks said. He wanted the ramrod to loosen up. It worked. Qualls chuckled. "Shad was closest to them. They shot my horse out from under me, but Shad cut down on a couple braves and covered me while I dived into some rocks. I hit one of 'em while Shad was joinin' me. We cleared three more of their ponies, an' Shad clubbed an Indian off his mustang. They vanished into the draw. We pulled out on Shad's horse, looked back, saw 'em come back to get their dead."

"If redskins try to hit us," said Qualls, "we'll have to be ready. We've got some good beef, and some of those Indians are hungry if their hunting has been meager. We can give away a few head we brought along in case. Help the hungry, sure, but not give up the herd." He lifted the rifle that lay across his pommel. He'd made sure every rider was well-armed. Heavy cartridge belts were looped around all the men's waists.

The third day ended and the fourth began, then the fifth. The spot where they bedded the longhorns on the fifth day was a grassy meadow between long hills northwest of Trinidad. Flanking the bedding area to the north a small creek spilled out of a canyon, fringed with cottonwoods, willows, and wild plums. The cattle relished the thick grass as well as the water.

For three days, the riders had gotten glimpses of the two Spanish Peaks off to the north and somewhat west. For a long time they had been called the *Huajatolla*, "the breasts of the world." They had been guiding marks for ancient tribes, Spanish conquérors, early trappers and traders, and military expeditions. They also beckoned permanent settlers who began to dig out farms and build adobes or log cabins in the late 1850s and early 1860s.

Already weary from the hard, twisting trek on the Raton slopes, some of the men wolfed down fresh beef, pinto beans, biscuits, and molasses "lick." They savored hot coffee against the chilling night wind that swept down across the meadow. Then they rode off on fresh horses to take the patrols of riders who had not yet eaten. Those not on duty lingered over the supper more at leisure. They exchanged cow talk, yarns about trails of the past, or played cards. Some of them listened as Marks read a few pages from a book out of his saddlebag, *Scenes of Rocky Mountain Life* by Rufus Sage, written in the late 1840s.

Marks got up, threw more pine on the fire, and came back to relish a warm jolt of coffee. A cold wind caressing the meadow caused him to pull up his shirt and coat collars. He heard the rider on the near side of the sleeping longhorns singing to the animals. The man drew closer as his horse carried him on his rounds.

"Smiley," Hap explained, detecting an interest in Marks's face by the pale light of the flames. "Best singin' cowboy I ever heard. Oughta be one o' them stage singers in Denver. Even sings some o' the hymns I used to hear Ma sing back in Tennessee. Never had much chance to go to a church 'ceptin' when I was just a wart. Churches jest don't seem to be where I am. Just a circuit rider once in a while. But I used to enjoy goin', an' I got a lift from the songs, 'specially the way Ma sang 'em and lived 'em."

"Been myself." Marks smiled. The voice out there lifted on the words of "Rock of Ages." He added: "I liked it too. Hypocrites mixed in at times, but more of the best kind of folk. I found out that the right kind of believing, the kind Pa and Ma had, made sense. It added up in the way *they* lived it, too. Genuine, simple, shining. The right kind, mind you. Nothing weak or sissified about it. I always felt tryin' to go the Lord's way made me stronger."

"Yeah, it does." Hap carefully sewed up a shirt he'd ripped. "I see that, the pure-quill religion, in the Spellmans. Real down to earth, God-fearin' stock. You always get a fair deal with them."

"For sure." Marks's mind took wings and flew back to Jackie, to the daguerreotype picture of the girl named Mandie, to his sister, Becky. "Nobody has to drag me to that kind of livin'."

"Nor me," Hap shook his head. "I've changed my thinkin' a lot since I was a towhead. Thought I was bein' smart an' big to say I didn't have need of it. But I got on friendly terms with the Lord a few years ago. Plan to keep it that way. After all, he made me, gave me life, hears my prayers right along. Man would be a fool to strike out on his own." He went on with his mending. Cowboys often patched their own clothes, or some had a handy cook do it. "Smiley's one o' them folk I cotton to. One o' the cleanest livin' men I ever knowed. Always tries to help, like he was there to save the Scovil lady. Never uppity 'bout his beliefs. But his beliefs work. Never heard him cuss, or do any spite to one o' the men. Cheerful through the tough times.

"But you know, sometime, maybe not far back, Smiley's been hurt. Some woman, I'd wager. Got stung twice myself. Once on a Mississippi riverboat, 'nother time at a stagecoach inn down in San Antonio. Stung bad. Both times, they played up to me, then dumped me when someone else came along with more money. I can read sign in other men, too. There are many good women, like the lady Spellman. But some of 'em can really hurt a man. Anyhow, that's one subject Smiley clams up on. Jest meditates, or walks off.

"But wasn't that somethin' wonderful he did for Miss Scovil out by the herd? I tell you, whoever the woman was that hurt him, if she could've been *that* woman, maybe she'd be of a different mind now."

Marks, oiling his Colt .44, looked up thoughtfully. He heard Smiley's stanza drift away on the circuit. Another rider, meeting Smiley, was singing a soothing lullaby to the longhorns.

"Maybe," he murmured. He'd been so busy before and during the drive that he had not given much thought to Uncle Hu Scovil, his beautiful black-haired niece, and the taunting Tontam. Now his mind galloped back as Hap went for a walk. He mulled over the rush of events. Back flashed the chase that the trio from Colorado said was a race. He saw again the fear that crossed Miss Voni's face like a dark shadow; the way she was cowed before Scovil and Tontam and yielded to whatever they ordered; her sullen silence at times during meals. She could cover up in part by her Uncle Hu's constant gab, especially when he spoke up instantly for her. But the mean threat in the corner bedroom came back.

Marks sensed that something was badly wrong in the Scovil family, something sinister between Scovil and Tontam. It was like a burr under the saddle of his mind. He couldn't seem to let it go.

Chat died down around the fire. But a gentle breeze touched the men's cheeks and carried on its breath the soothing melody of Smiley.

Marks's thoughts returned to himself, Jeanie, and Jackie. He remembered the surprise. Yonder it waited in his saddlebag near the rear wagon wheel. It was to be opened when alone. He got up and looked around for a place to saunter off from the men.

Qualls's commanding voice nailed him in his tracks.

"All right, men, that's it. You'll get precious little sleep. So hit it. You'll be relievin' others 'fore you know it, or Jawbone will be singin' 'Rise an' shine.' Pleasant dreams."

The surprise would have to tease Marks's mind till another day. He dozed, but it seemed that he had hardly closed his eyes. Then he leaped to his knees. One of the most bloodcurdling screams he had ever heard shattered the night air. In an instant the cattle sprang to their feet, snorting, sniffing, bellowing, and milling in an uneasy mass. Marks and the others put on their hats, trousers, and shirts and scrambled to horses that Qualls had had them keep saddled.

A great fear laid its talon grip on them. Any second

that tossing sea of beef could explode like a tidal wave through the night. And in this terrain of ridges and plains that most of the riders did not know, anything could happen.

7

Men riding night herd were desperate to lull the frightened animals back into quietness. They were singing calming words. Cowboys who had leaped out of their blankets joined them, calling out to the cattle in familiar voices. Nobody seemed to know who had screamed or why. Rifles played on the dark line of the trees along the brook. At the slightest movement the outfit would be ready. But they were caught between two impulses: shoot in self-defense, or hold off lest gunfire stampede eight thousand hooves and the remuda to boot.

"Hap, Marks, come with me." It was the bark of Qualls, surging through the darkness. The ramrod lifted his horse to a fast walk around the seething cattle. The scream had issued from over by a cluster of cottonwoods. There, dark masses of growth along the stream would furnish cover for an enemy's advance on the herd.

Indians? Coe's bunch? The Klugger gang?

One fact puzzled all of the riders: Only one scream had blasted on the quiet meadow that now churned like a boiling pot. Yet an ominous stillness lay across the hills and in the ravines. To the west a ridge hovered darkly as if to witness how the drovers would deal with the crisis.

Was that scream meant to trigger the cattle into a run?

The two trail hands fell in with their segundo, rifles poised and eyes probing at the blackness. Any moment a burst of deadly gunfire from the threatening depths could whack down Qualls and his men. And that could discharge the spooked herd into two thousand nocturnal cannonballs.

If those cattle did erupt, the herd would become a churning, heaving mass thundering pell-mell over a broken land to the north, south, or east. And it might mean death to some animals and some men. Before them would be boulders, trees, deadly slashes in the earth, unexpected rises. The riders moved with their hearts in their throats. A sickening dread clutched at the pits of their stomachs. It is one thing to advance in broad daylight when the enemy is in sight or their rifles are flashing over boulders or an adobe fortress. It is another to tear into the black cave of night and possible death.

The three horsemen reached the north side of the herd. As yet, the cattle had not shot into a bovine avalanche. Wile Gaster took shape, looming up in the darkness like a monster on his horse.

"Smiley an' Chip sallied over for a look-see," he reported to Qualls. " 'Tuther side of the crick. Smiley heard a horse pullin' out at a run. One horse, he thought."

Smiley splashed his mustang back across the tiny, gurgling creek, meeting Qualls and the others.

"Seems we've had a visit from at least one hombre," he announced. "I never heard a worse scream. Then a poundin' noise, like a man was slappin' his hand on a rock. Then some sputterin' gasps that made my blood run cold. After that boots runnin' in the sand, an' a horse runnin'."

"Fan out an' find his tracks," Qualls commanded. "Get every clue."

A couple of minutes later, Chip recoiled from a pile of rocks. The others heard his gasp. "Wow-eeeeee!" A moment later he said, "Here's the story. Have a look."

When the others had converged, Chip struck a match, holding it down beside a large rock. In the flicker they saw a four-foot rattler writhing its very last.

Marks, peering down, saw the bloody, battered-in head. Blood was splattered on rocks within the circle of light. But his keen eyes observed something further. "Look here." He drew their attention, hunkering down and pointing more closely to the fangs.

"Ow-w-w-w-w," Qualls rasped. A grimace leaped along his leathery features in the flare of another match. "Tore out some of the man's skin and some flesh. So. That was it. The man was layin' low, bellyin' in to spy on the herd. This other slitherin' snake is out later in the fall than rattlers usually are, but I've known some later than this. It hit him 'fore he knew it was there."

"Yeah. He must've grabbed the rattler an' tried to jerk it loose," Smiley surmised. They shuddered. It was obvious that the spy had beaten the rattler against the rock rather than flinging it into the brush.

Marks dragged another match across the rock to light it. He knelt to focus the brightness closer to the portion of torn human skin. "Worse thing was, it hit him right in the face or neck." He laid a thumbnail across some long fibers of hair.

"Well, poor critter won't last far," Hap said grimly.

Sure enough, they came across the man's body sprawled atop a mat of sagebrush. It lay less than a quarter of a mile down the hills. Tracks in a lantern's light revealed that when the man plunged off his mount, the animal lunged on through the night.

" 'Pears this one was scoutin' us out," said Qualls. "He was to report back. So, his sidekicks must have a camp not far off. Some of us will follow these tracks. I'm anxious to see who's so interested in our herd. Maybe it's Coe's bunch from Robbers' Roost."

"I'll volunteer, boss." It was Marks. "Trackin' is one thing I like to do. Learned it from my family an' a couple of Indians."

"I believe you." Qualls nodded. "You got sand, kid. If it wasn't for you, I wouldn't be here. Only I don't want any harm to come to you. I want your pa and ma to see you comin' home some day."

"I'm obliged," Marks returned. "But I've taken risks all the way from Texas—risks right along with the others. I know you're a man to feel the same for every man Jack in your outfit. There's nothin' special about me, above the rest. Count me in, an' I'd be grateful."

The ramrod sat his saddle for a moment. Marks knew he was thinking it over. He felt the boss's eyes studying him in the darkness.

"You've got it," said Qualls. "All right, Hap an' Smiley, too. Marks, go fetch a horse we can tote this hombre on, then we'll be on our way. Make it pronto."

A short time later, after they stuck with the horse tracks for what they guessed to be a couple of miles, they caught up with the animal. It had stopped to graze near the mouth of a canyon. The riderless horse had snapped the long-worn reins by tromping on them and jerking up.

"Must've been so spooked by the scream and the man tumblin' off that he hit these at a run and popped 'em off," said Qualls.

They hooked the man's broad belt on the horn and bound it fast with cords. They also tied the body into the saddle seat so that it could not slide any direction even if slumped over the saddle bow. Then they got the horse moving and followed for another couple of miles northward. Finally the mount veered westward into another canyon. A cold breeze, sending shivers through them, bore a scent of piñon smoke.

The horse went on along the canyon. The clippity-clop of his hooves striking rocks and dust would fall on the ears of those at the camp. It was just a matter of time. A moment passed, then another. The horse plodded on steadily, carrying the dead man. Then the four who pursued heard a raucous laugh. When that laugh died on the midnight air, another voice cut in.

"Someone's comin'." That slapped a hush on the camp except for the scurry of boots rushing to reach positions in case of trouble.

"Comin' slow," a voice spoke into the night. Then, hopefully, "Gart's due in. That you, Gart?"

No answer.

The horse, anxious to get to the other horses about thirty yards short of the camp fire, came only to the very pale fringe of light. There he halted. His rider slumped very low over the mane and front shoulder in an odd way.

One of the men edged out of the darkness, his rifle

ready for action. He pulled up the head of the dead man toward the fire and squinted, unable to see clearly.

"My Gawd, he's dead! Gart's dead!"

"Injuns?" somebody hissed from back in the shadows.

Not yet aware that the dead rider was tied on, the man lifted the body higher on the horse's shoulder. The belt slipped over and off the horn and Gart slid sideways a little. Rawhide held him.

"How's it look?" another voice inquired from brush and rocks. "Bullets . . . or Injun arrers?"

Puzzling at getting Gart's body loose and wondering if he had hooked himself on to make it back, the man with the corpse scratched a match into flame. The first thing he saw was Gart's face. That seized his attention. He yelped like a coyote, then cursed.

"Well, what is it?" a voice demanded from hiding.

"Gart—he—he's been snakebit! Ahhhhhhhh! Right in the jaw. Fang marks!"

"Yer funnin' me."

"Naw. See fer your own self. Ahhhhhhhh! I can't look no more." The match flame went out. Ten aroused and curious men converged on the horse and body.

During this drama to investigate the fate of the outlaw, four stealthy figures slipped into positions. Hap and Smiley crept to the far side of the men gathering to the horse, sprawling behind cover about fifteen feet apart. Qualls bellied down about ten feet to the left of the victim's horse just after two men left their hiding spots. And Marks stole in, hidden by the picketed horses, dropping on his knees behind a juniper.

Qualls's voice thundered. "You're covered from every side! Throw up yore hands."

Heads jerked around, bodies froze, and gasps leaped from tongues. The men were gripped by panic. They did not know who would take burning lead first. After the startled grunts, hands began to steal toward six-shooters.

"Forget the guns, or this'll be yore graveyard," Hap cut in. "Yo're lined in a crisscross. One wrong move an' you'll be riddled."

Hands lifted away from the weapons stubbornly but surely. A great uncertainty gripped the camp. If, indeed, men had them trapped from every side, they could be dead before they clawed their guns clear. They stood dumbfounded. Hands stretched toward the stars, but eyes darted this way and that.

"The herd," Qualls prodded. "What's your interest in our herd?"

A big blond tried to peer into the blackness at the voice. "Whatta yuh mean, the herd?" he fumbled.

"You know, yeller hair. We caught yore man Gart spyin' on the cattle. But a snake stopped him, an' he led us here. We've got you linked with a hombre that tried to do me in. Another polecat, Ike Klugger. One of you killed him to make sure he wouldn't squeal. We get impatient with any that have plans for another man's cattle."

"Ahhhhh," Gatril sighed. His voice took on a tone of incredulity. "You figger us all wrong. Ike, he ain't been with us for a long time. Last we heard he'd drifted over to join the Coe gang, somers near Madison Emory's place. Now Ike rilin' you this way, I don't blame you. I'd be mad too. But there ain't no connection any more between Ike an' us."

"You lie through yore teeth," Hap threw in. "You

an' two o' yore breed were at Cimarron. Our men saw you go into Swink's, an' you were with Ike. No mistake. Then three o' you tried to lay yore paws on a girl—Katie Sutter—ridin' to fetch help for her ma when she was in pain to deliver. Our men tracked you toward Raton Pass."

Gatril dropped his chin on his chest in a shrug of resignation. He let out a great gust of air. His men shifted uneasily, laying a waiting glance on him. Each sought a trail out of trouble.

"We mean to put you off our trail," Qualls said stiffly. "We'll start with you droppin' those gun belts, nice an' easy. Make even a move that looks sneaky, an' we'll drop you on the spot. Off with 'em—now!"

Sullenly the ten obeyed, casting nervous glances into the inky darkness. Then Qualls snapped a command for them to belly down in the sand, spread-eagled. Smiley moved in cautiously and gathered the gun belts and rifles he saw about the camp. Then he went from one man to another, checking them from boots to hats for concealed weapons. He came up with two revolvers tucked inside coats, a derringer from a shoulder holster on Gatril, a derringer from a boot on another outlaw, and several kinds of knives. Laying his collection in a pile over by the horses, he also shucked the rifles from the saddles.

"Now," said Qualls, "you can sit up. Sit, I said. We'll talk about yore fate." Hap tossed more wood on the fire. The foreman went on. "We could string you all by the necks from one of these canyon rims back here, or find a high limb. We'd be rid of a pack of trouble. Or we might set you afoot an' take all yore guns. Let the Utes have at you."

"Hold it!" one of the outlaws blurted out. "Seven of

us, me, Hacker, Tyson, an' others, we never had nothin' to do with no Cimarron business."

Gatril, the squat hombre, and a hook-nosed man glared at the speaker.

"That won't wash," Qualls shot back harshly. "Yo're with 'em *now*. Yore man was spyin' out the herd. You bought into trouble. You got the same ticket, you get the same show."

Marks had been studying Gatril's face closely and was sure he recognized it from one of the wanted posters he'd seen. He puzzled for a second over the name, then suddenly remembered it—Gatril.

"First," said Marks, "I'd like to know how Gatril an' his bunch got wind of this drive an' drifted a long way from Texas just at the right time, with Klugger."

Gatril was unnerved at having Marks recognize him, but he gave no acknowledgment that the young drover was correct.

"Yeah," Smiley chimed in. "That's a good question."

Hacker, the man who had wanted a way out for himself and the other two, started to say something. But Gatril laid the back of his big hand to the mouth of Hacker quickly.

"No, Hacker, it might as well be me that explains. You see, it was like this." He jerked a thumb toward the rattler's victim. "Gart, he rode for the Scovil ranch east o' Fountain Crick, north of the Arkansas. He got wind o' the Scovils buyin' cattle. Most of us had drifted north from the Brazos, an' we was hard up, I mean hungry. We figgered if we took a steer, jest one, it wouldn't hurt much. We'd be able to eat."

"You lie like the devil hisself," Qualls snorted. "You were after the whole herd. You sent Ike to take me out o' the picture, permanent. An' I reckon one o' you cut Spellman's cinch strap an' got him busted up for months. You figger *that* wouldn't hurt much?"

"Well, thet was Ike's doin', strictly his'n. Ike, he was one to go whole hog. An' Ike, he had his enemies. We figgered one of 'em heard Ike was at Cimarron an' lit onto his trail. Could be someone from Coe's wild bunch. I tell you, thet's gospel."

"The devil's kind," Marks growled.

Qualls dragged a watch from his denim pocket and saw the time was nearly one in the morning. "Time's wastin'," he said sharply. "I've made up my mind. You hombres have lied. So you'll get what's comin'."

"Huh, whatta you mean?" Hacker was close to panic. Visions of a cottonwood limb and an ominous noose flitted before his eyes.

"You'll find yore horses, pistols, and knives at the cottonwoods where the herd bedded down. That is, if Utes haven't found them first. The walk ought to impress on you that we mean business. The herd goes through. We keep yore rifles. So you won't try any long-range work on us. We'll move the herd out at sunup. An' you'd better not come for your things till we're gone. My men will be under orders to shoot first, ask questions later. Get that? An' when you climb on yore horses, head south for Trinidad or back to Texas. You come our way an' you'll run into more trouble than you bargained for. Another thing: When you leave the cottonwoods, I'll have men watchin'. You won't see them, but they'll see you. You show any contrary notion, an' they'll cut loose with rifles at a range you can't match. You won't stand a lobo's chance in a shootin' gallery. Do I make myself clear?"

"Man, thet ain't human." The squat man sputtered and leered out of hate-filled eyes.

"I can make it worse," Qualls shot back. He'd had enough of stinking polecats for one night. He knew he was letting them off relatively easy. "An' who said I need to be human to a den o' snakes? Yo're gettin' my point muy pronto."

"But—but thet's miles back to the crick by the cottonwoods," Hawk Mangis informed the ramrod. His hair-choked lips had sagged open like a small cave, his face showing pain.

"I figgered you knew exactly where the herd is," Qualls drawled.

"But if Injuns hit us on the way, without our pistols even, we won't stand a chance."

"That, friend hawk-nose, is true." Qualls' lips were drawn tightly. "I'd wager, then, that you wouldn't make it. Save someone the job of a hangin' later, if you don't change yore ways."

8

Frank Spellman had seldom felt sheer pain rack his body as he had since the nasty spill. Doc Tilden said he'd broken his left leg and cracked several ribs. Healing would require several weeks, even months.

But Spellman, like Lucien Maxwell at Cimarron and Shoat Hartman on his ranch near Rayado, could take what the West dealt at its roughest.

Comfort from Jeanie and Jackie was soothing. This jewel of a woman Jeanie, who had come westward in a wagon train to see the ranch he'd sought out, was an elixir to his heart. She did her work, washing on the scrub board, ironing with heated flat irons, cooking, cleaning the house, mending. And she and Jackie were still unpacking. These chores and a hundred other things kept her going. But she found time—*made* time—to sit by his bedside and simply be his companion. The love of years was in her heart, deeper than ever. Side by side with Frank she had grappled with the rigors of the frontier when he had been a marshal. And she did not flinch now but offered her husband the best tonic, a warming smile and a tender voice that relieved the torture and charged him with new will to live.

He laid his Bible on a table and opened it to Proverbs 31, the description of a virtuous woman. "*That* woman," he sighed toward heaven, "lives in my home."

And Jackie was already getting a lot like her ma. Jeanie had not forgotten the elegance, grace, and polish of her upbringing in faraway Georgia. She had improved it and taught it to her daughter. And with it Jeanie added a healthy dash of spice from her strong inward character. It was a blessing of cheering love, of brightening joyousness, of serenity before the Almighty. He was her special friend.

Jeanie sat with Frank today, the fourth day since the herd had tromped northeastward across the grass.

The rancher was grateful, amidst his pain every time he turned, that she gave him generously and gladly of her time. Then she worked the harder to finish necessary chores when away from his bedside.

She had been reading some of William Shakespeare's plays and a book by Lewis Garrard about his experiences in the Colorado and New Mexico territories in the late 1840s. She had just finished a section by Garrard on a trip past Vermejo Creek and through the Sangre de Cristo Mountains to Taos, and back. Now she laid the book aside and covered part of his rugged hand with her soft fingers.

"Well, at least you listened this time," she chided. "Before your mind was somewhere else. With the herd and with the men. North of Wootton's tollgate in the pass, maybe beyond Trinidad. I'll bet they saw the Spanish Peaks beckoning yesterday and today."

"Yes, Jeanie. Qualls knows how to take the cattle steadily on, but never too fast. I think if I had one ounce of strength more'n I've got, I'd slap my gear on a horse an' burn the trail to catch them. I keep wonderin' about Indians, about the rustlin' pack Gatril leads, an' about grass an' water. Then there's Coe's outlaws—could be a big outfit. You know the reports of them stealin' horses an' cattle and robbin' trains on the Santa Fe Trail."

"Yes," she replied softly. "But Frank, we've got to rest in the trust that God will help us. And Bart knows what he's doin'. I know from things he's said that Bart is trusting in the Lord. A finer trail boss never took a herd out. And you yourself said he's got an outfit that can back him up. They don't come any more capable than Hap, Wile, Smoky, and our new man, Smiley. They're almost as good as Shoat Hartman's bunch."

"I know, I know," he agreed. "An' Marks, too. Still a kid in years he may be. But Jeanie, he's grown up already, the beginnings of a man's man. He did us one tall favor, savin' Bart's life. A Dunlee he is. We all saw the calibre of man Lonan is. He stopped Duke Maskill an' rescued me from the hidden gorge. An' I'll never forget the Dunlees' pa, Buckskin. A man of principle, a man of flint."

"And so gentle." She repeated words Frank had told her before.

"Yes, an' so gentle." He gazed away, his mind taking long strides like a great stallion back through the years. Buckskin had come tearing in at breakneck speed to give him a ride out of that Comanche trap, arrows flying all about. Reaching safety, he'd doctored Frank with the patience and gentleness of a softhearted nurse. He was one man who had shown that manly strength, courage, and prowess with horse or gun could mingle with a heart tuned to the good Lord. Buckskin whetted the appetites of others to follow him and be that kind of man too. "Lonan said Marks has savvy like an Indian in scoutin' out water, or handlin' hisself in an attack."

"Himself, dear," she corrected gently, and smiled.

"Himself. Ah, I know, Jeanie. When'll I ever learn them proper words?" A grin climbed the lengths of his cheeks which she had shaved for him that morning. "Anyhow, I don't doubt the men can handle things. Don't doubt it. Still, restlessness stirs in me. I crave to be there, feel the bite of the wind in my face, look out across the sea of backs bobbin' like the waves on a ripplin' lake, watch those longhorns pour through a canyon, smell the bacon sizzlin' at Jawbone's fire, face everything the men face."

"Well do I know that," Jeanie said. She took up Garrard's book *Wah-to-yah and the Taos Trail*, held it open like a fan, and whipped the air near her husband's face. That gave him a bit of refreshment. Then she reached over, took a wet cloth from a basin of cool water, and spread it over his forehead. A touch of the fever still worked within him. He was grateful for the coolness. "It's been so quiet since Bart and the others moved them out. And our guests have gone. I'll have to get busy on that quilt. We'll need another one this winter."

"You need company," Frank said. "I can get one o' the men to ride into town, an' bring Emilie out to visit. Even when Matt's daughter was here, you didn't get much of a chance to visit."

"No, that was kind of strange," she mused. "I still don't know what to make of it. She offered to help wash the dishes the first night. But then she went to her room and stayed. Her uncle had talked with her. She never even offered to help again. Oh, it's not the helping or not helping. Something seemed to be eating at the girl. Then I overheard her crying in her room, crying as if her heart would break. I asked if I could help. She just said, 'Oh, no, it's something I can't talk about.' Now what do you suppose?"

"Probably it's about her pa," he offered. "Him bein' shot in the back. You know, some folk react in a more sensitive way than others, an' they cry it out. Or maybe it's just that her uncle Hu is a mite overbearin'."

"That may be it, or part of it," she agreed. "I caught her uncle giving her the eye. It was like he didn't want her to speak up. Some men are like that. They think the women an' the younger folk are only to be seen now and then, not to be heard. And do you suppose that man Tontam could be trying to make his job as bodyguard *more* than just that? I don't see how any girl could stand for him to get near." She shuddered.

"Tontam makes the hair stand up on the back o' your neck, all right," the rancher agreed. "Calloused as a rattler, an' besides that a struttin' peacock, proud to the point of tauntin' people for the cussedness of it. But Hu Scovil swears he's one of the best with a gun. He feels he an' the girl will be safe with Tontam around. Let's just hope Hu hisself will always be close if Miss Voni needs him."

Jeanie gazed through the window to the east. The herd had vanished over there. Then she thought of the west. "The two men Hack Griner's sending to help us should be riding over tomorrow."

"Yeah. That'll lift a weight. I know I don't have any special cause to worry, but I keep thinkin' about the money Hu Scovil paid down—one-third—with the rest due when the cattle reach Matt's ranch. More'n twenty thousand dollars. He insisted on payin' cash, greenbacks. Well, it's laid away in that satchel in the desk drawer. If anybody tried to take it he'd have to get by me." He laid his fingers on the butt of the Colt revolver lying in its holster on the bunk beside him. "Still, I'll rest easier when Hack's men get here. An' Hack'll come along to get his cut for the cattle he sent."

Both of the Spellmans reflected on the safety since the day before the herd moved out, since the ambush laid for Qualls and the bushwhacking of the ambusher himself. There had not been a ripple against the usual life of the ranch.

"I reckon," Frank told his wife, "as I have all along. The danger lies with the *herd*. It's one thing to cut a cinch or throw down on a man alone miles out in the hills. It's another to come right into an outfit's headquarters an' try a robbery. I know those three tried it years ago when I was marshal. But that was very unusual." He slid his Colt from its scabbard. "You know what happened when they tried to rob us."

Yes, she remembered well. It had happened just before dark. While the two ranch dogs they had then had gone with one of the cowboys on a rabbit hunt, three men had slipped inside the house. Frank was sprawled on the living room floor with a headache. A marshal as well as a small rancher then, he lived on hair-trigger vigilance. He detected the creak of a floorboard, sensed that it sounded stealthy, and drew his gun.

When the men eased into the room, Frank had the pistol trained on them. One man tried to duck back, and threw up his six-shooter. But he took a slug in the arm and dropped the weapon. The three men tore out of the house, but Spellman, quick as a cougar, brought them to a halt in the yard.

They went to jail and later left the area. Jeanie reflected on all of this and on the steel-tough man Frank was. But she realized that her husband was not able to do what he had done then. She went to the kitchen, took a revolver off a shelf, checked the load, and laid it inside a big pocket of her apron.

Loop and Tack, she knew, were on the alert as they worked around the barn and corrals. When one rode to check the nearer ranges where cattle grazed, the other was doubly watchful.

The family ate supper. Then Jeanie went out to pull weeds in the vegetable garden behind the house. She touched the revolver lightly through the apron and was reassured. Loop and Tack, as she had just told Frank, sat on the bunkhouse steps, smoking and looking toward the house. Frequently they both walked about in the ranch yard or out from the buildings and corrals, alert for any sign of visitors.

Jackie was sprawled across her bed reading. Frank lay on his bunk in the front room off the kitchen, the desk with the money beyond him near the far wall. He was glad to be in the front room where he could see the front door and watch the windows.

Two riders with hoods over their heads and shoulders tied their horses in piñons well back behind the garden at the back of the house. They had walked their horses in slowly, making no noise that would carry. One man patiently crawled through brush as high as his thighs, reaching the rear wall of the bunkhouse by a corral. He knew there was a dog, and made sure the breeze was blowing toward him, not allowing his scent to carry. Calling on the utmost stealth, he crept along the corral side end of the bunkhouse. Peering around the corner, he saw the two ranch hands smoking and petting the new ranch dog, a German shepherd named "Coffee."

Then the intruder edged back around the cowboy quarters to a window that was open to admit fresh air. He climbed through with painstaking care to be quiet. Any slight sound that the dog otherwise might detect would be hidden by the rustle of the breeze in a cotton-wood brushing against the bunkhouse. After tiptoeing across the hard-packed dirt floor, making certain he did not bump a bunk or some other object, he reached a spot near the door. Searching the semidarkness, he spied an empty tin bucket on a table. He dragged rags from a pocket and lit them, then dropped the burning cloth into the bucket.

Loop Sorrels finished a cigarette and ground the stub into the dust with his boot heel. "Time to scout around agin," he said.

"Hey, what's goin' on?" Tack Laycox exclaimed, sniffing and looking all around. "Smoke! I smell smoke." Mystified, he was ready to rush out where he could command a wider view of the ranch area. "Comin' from inside," Loop judged. "Did we leave a cigarette burnin'?" They wheeled. Smoke issued from the crack in the door, which was open only a foot or so. They bolted in to put out the fire.

Suddenly they were gaping into the mouth of a Colt .44.

The man in the hood ordered them to drop on their stomachs, then took their shooting irons. Smothering his fire, he hastily bound their ankles and wrists and jammed gags into their mouths. He'd knotted rocks in those gags to hold firmly inside their mouths. That done, he glanced and saw the dog lying about thirty feet out in the yard. Suspicious, the shepherd was emitting a low growl. The hooded man took a package from his coat. He shook from it a chunk of beef he had "doctored," and tossed it to the dog without showing his body.

Coffee leaped away, then came back to sniff warily. He was tantalized by the scent of something he liked. Overcome, he went at the meat with intensity. Though it had gathered some dust, he'd make a short meal of it. The invader waited. It did not take long. Coffee lay stretched in a deep doze, out of the action.

A second man stalked in from behind the garden. Jeanie Spellman was pulling weeds and watching around her. But she did not see the man until he raised up from the brush at the edge of the garden. Shocked, she dropped a weed and straightened up. The first thought that stabbed her mind was that he was a Ute or an Apache. She'd frequently seen them near the ranch, but they had done no harm. She'd set out a bucket of milk and a loaf of bread several times, and these had always been taken, the bucket returned.

The murky gray of twilight was upon her, but she could see he was not a Ute or Apache in white man's clothes. She knew from his voice he was a white man, disguised in a hood.

"Not a sound, lady." The voice was a low rasp, very thick and strained. The man aimed a pistol at her. "We have your husband, so don't try to be a hero." He came to her half-hunched over, a big man. "Walk to the door, and quiet! Right to your husband, an' I'm close behind. I hear you have a daughter. Just hope she doesn't get in the way."

Cold stabs of fear cut through Jeanie, but she fumbled out words. "We—we've got ranch hands. They'll stop you."

"Naw, they're out of it. We took care o' that. Now, get along, an' don't let out a peep." He reached inside the pocket of her apron, his fingers closed on a pistol, and he lifted it out.

They reached the back door. Jeanie led the way inside. An awful pounding assaulted her heart. She had let Frank and Jackie down—worked too late and not been vigilant enough.

"Tell your man you want to show him some things from the garden," the man ordered in a deep growl. Something unnatural about his voice disturbed her. He prodded her with the pistol, none too gently. She stepped into the house, walked briefly along a short hallway past a bedroom, then stepped into the front room where Frank lay. She was trying to hit on some way to warn Frank, something obvious to him.

"Frank," she tried to put into her voice the tone he would know spelled fear. Then something else. "I—I looked at the young apple trees you planted." Maybe he would get his hand on his Colt revolver under the sheets.

Frank blinked in the light of a lamp he had fumbled to light a few minutes before. Apple trees? He'd only *promised* to plant them. As Jeanie stepped into the room, his fingers slid toward the revolver.

"Don't touch it!" A gruff voice lashed the room. It cut like the sharp edge of a bullwhip Frank had seen vaqueros use in the brush thickets of the Nueces strip where longhorns hid out. The rancher's fingers stopped. He winced, tried to sit up, and gritted his teeth at the piercing pain that racked his ribs and leg. In the pale glow of the lamp he gazed at the deadly snout of a Colt revolver threatening his chest.

"Oh, no," he groaned. Now a pain shot through his frame even worse than the hurt of a broken body. Again he considered the gun lying with butt toward him—close, yet so far away. He could not move with that speed he'd had as a marshal.

"Frank, I'm sorry," Jeanie said, trembling. She fought back a sob. "I should have been more careful."

The hooded man stalked over and grabbed the gun away.

"What is it you want?" the rancher demanded.

"Money. You sold cattle. Common knowledge. No banks here. Money has to be around. Maxwell keeps money in his bureau drawer. I want that money, fast!"

Frank looked away from the desk over by the end wall. Could he stall for time? Loop and Tack—where were they? Could they be closing in?

Jeanie was ten feet from a rifle rack along the front wall. How much time would it take to reach a rifle, lift it from the elk antlers, load, and shoot? She knew Frank kept cartridges in the rifles, ready for fast action should Utes or Apaches intend harm.

"You! Woman! Get the money." The low, mean voice was urgent. Just then a second hooded figure stepped in from the front door.

"Go see to their daughter," the first man commanded. He kept his voice down so that it hardly carried across the one room. "Over there, try that room. There's another over here." The far bedroom door was near the back wall of the front room.

Jackie had listened to the music box Marks brought. Then she lay on her bed reading, after which she became lost in a girl's thoughts. She hoped Marks and the other riders were safe. But most of all she longed for Josh, the man she wanted to marry.

She got up, knelt beside the bed, and prayed. Pa came first in that brief prayer, then Josh and the trail drovers. Then she arose and went to sit on a stool by the window where she could see Ma out in the garden. Her eyes shifted to the dark line of hills to the north. Somewhere beyond the men would be camping with the cattle.

"I wonder," she mused, as she looked back at the music box, "if Marks has opened his surprise sack."

After her pleasant thoughts she was vaguely aware that Ma was coming in. But she scarcely noticed her out of a corner of her eye. Then the faintest murmur came to her ears. Was that a voice? Was Ma talking to Coffee? Or was Tack or Loop out there? She looked just in time. It was a man, and in his hand he held a gun!

Aroused from her daydreaming, she fled to a drawer. Fumbling, she got a revolver. Pa had taught her how to use it when she was much younger. It was already loaded. She opened her door quietly, just enough to peer around it into the front room. What she saw wrenched a gasp from her, but she smothered it. A cold, sickening feeling clutched her deeply in the stomach. A hooded man menaced Pa with a gun. She had not seen Pa's face, but she had seen Ma's. It was a study in fear.

Easing back, she pulled the door very softly closed.

She had to think, to do something, fast. Loop and Tack—where were they? Was there but one man with a gun, or were there others? She glanced at the window. An idea seized her mind. She heard boot heels thudding, approaching her room. Any second the door would open. She reached the window and went through it, glad she had opened it earlier to get a breeze. Dropping to the ground, she scurried softly along the edge of the wall. Inside, she heard her door yanked open. Then those dreadful boot heels again, invading her room.

Fairly flying, she got around the far corner. Then she stopped and peered back. A man's head and shoulders were thrust out the window to gaze outside. He, too, was hooded.

Looking toward the front yard, her eyes probed for Loop or Tack. She saw no cigarette glow in the semi-darkness. They had not yet lit a lantern in the bunkhouse. Strange. They might be out in the barn or corrals looking at some stock. Too far away.

Then her anxious eyes glimpsed the still form of Coffee. The dog was sleeping a few feet from the bunkhouse door.

"Coffee!" she scolded in a whisper, and stomped her foot. She'd believed him to be the fine watchdog Lucien Maxwell had vouched for when he gave him to the family.

Jackie hurried around the house, taking care to move quietly.

"Where's yore daughter?" demanded the man who had come back from Jackie's room.

Jeanie was relieved that she was not there. "Why, she must've slipped out for a walk." Jeanie had not been free to inch any closer to the rifle rack. That Winchester laid across the antler looked so promising.

Then a thought leaped through Jeanie's mind. Frank kept a pistol loaded in the same desk drawer where he'd stuck the satchel with the money. It was underneath the satchel, unseen, ready to be picked up with the satchel. She was frightened. Even should she divert the one man's attention, snatch that gun, and slip it out behind the satchel, she could not stop both men. And she could get Frank or herself or both of them killed.

"Where's the money? In that desk? Get over there." It was the first man's rasp. To his companion, he said, "Get outside. See if the girl's around."

Jeanie went to the desk and put her hand on the handle of the right drawer. Now that the second man had gone she might have a chance. Her frontier mind, always planning how to make do with what she had, hit on a scheme. She would reach both hands into the drawer, hiding the view from the man with her body. One hand had to close on the satchel, the other find the butt of the pistol, and a finger needed to find the trigger. She'd lift the gun out behind the satchel, as if grasping the satchel with both hands. It had to look natural, disarming. Then, before turning around, she must drop the hand with the pistol, keeping the gun hidden by her body, and hold it concealed behind the folds of her dress as she handed the satchel to the man. She trembled.

The second robber scanned the yard as he walked in a circle from the front door. He saw no sign of the girl. Impatient, he came back inside. The kitchen was to his left, an extension of the living room. Straight before him was a short hallway leading to the back door. He started toward that rear door, hoping he'd see the girl.

Right at that moment, Jackie leaned from the doorway he had just come through. At the slight sound, the returning thief spun. He was fast, but before he could jerk his gun up, the girl who already held a pistol poised pressed the trigger. A slug ripped along the left side of his shirt, seared a thin furrow along his rib cage, and thudded into the door behind his spinning body. His own bullet, fired in extreme haste, gouged wood out of the front doorpost. It would have meant death, but the girl had gotten off her shot and ducked back to safety.

The robber in the hallway crouched, wondering who had fired the shot. Had the ranch hands gotten loose? Or was the daughter shooting like this?

Before any shot had been fired, Jeanie's left hand extended the satchel to the other robber. She held it high, blocking his vision of her other hand. The man grabbed it, and started to open it to be sure it held a wad of greenbacks. When the two shots crashed inside the house, he almost jumped out of his skin. He wheeled and swung his gun around. Like a cornered wolf, he was ready to destroy.

The desk was a couple of feet from the wall, and Jeanie stepped back behind it. Her revolver swung over the top of the desk, gripped by both hands, and she searched for the target. The man with the satchel flung a glance back and saw her gun, then lurched sideways. Her pistol spat lead, peeling skin off the robber's knuckles. He fired by instinct, his bullet plowing a wicked furrow across the polished desk and drilling the plaster between stones.

Panicked that he could not see his target but was wide open, the man drove hard for the hallway. He sought the back door. His partner leaped out of the way of his hurling body, then bolted behind him.

Another shot from the front door took hair off the neck of the man behind. Then he lunged outside. Both hooded men raced through the garden and dug furiously for the brush and trees. They glanced back, triggering shots at the back door.

Jeanie darted to the antlers and snatched the rifle. Jackie, clutching her pistol, followed her ma to the rear door. But they heard bullets thudding into it and drew back. Then they dusted the fleeing robbers with bullets as they bolted into the piñons. Hoofbeats broke on the evening air as the two women hurried back to join Frank. He lay writhing in the hurt of cracked ribs and a busted leg. He had tried valiantly to reach the rack for another rifle. They helped him to his bunk. Then Jeanie swept Jackie in one arm, drawing her to the bedside.

"Thank God we're all alive!" She buried her face against Frank's shoulder, bursting into sobs. Presently she looked up. "Jackie, you're a brave girl—a true daughter of your pa."

"And my ma."

"What about Loop an' Tack?" Frank asked anxiously. "Find 'em. If they're all right, send one of 'em to Sheriff Stover. That money—we've got to get it back!"

Jeanie went out and returned quickly. "Loop and Tack were tied and gagged. Coffee's in a stupor. The robber used a smoke trick to lure the men into the bunkhouse. Then he threw some meat to Coffee. It must have been doped. Frank, Loop and Tack are sick that they didn't stop this."

Loop threw saddles on horses while Tack went into the piñons to see if he might make out a trail by lantern light.

"Jeanie," said Frank, "did you notice those men's

voices? Seemed artificial somehow. Like disguisin' how they really would talk."

"Yes, I noticed," she replied.

"It's men who were afraid their real voices would give them away," Frank said. "Must be some men we've met, who were sure we'd recognize their natural voices. But they could be any of a lot of people. Hard to believe they might be people we trust. Who are they?"

9

Qualls and his men rode wearily back to camp after the raid on the plotting rustlers. The men laid the extra rifles and ammunition in the chuck wagon and answered the questions of the drovers who had stuck with the herd.

Marks was proud of the way the ramrod had handled things. Qualls acted quickly and decisively. Spellman had a good man taking his and Griner's cattle north. This segundo cast a long shadow. Such a man's man took the youthful rider's mind back to his pa, Buckskin, and brothers Shaddo, Lonan, and Shiloh. He felt honored to ride with Qualls.

The strike into the outlaws' canyon camp had worn away some of the hours in the dark early morning. Jawbone would be rustling up breakfast in two or three hours. At the moment he had plenty of hot coffee waiting. Downing two cups of this, Qualls stood warming his back at the blazing fire. He was thankful that the men had gotten the longhorns quieted down. He flipped his tin cup into the tub and turned to speak to his men.

He told every man what to do. Then he turned to Marks. "Catch a bit o' shut-eye, kid. Then we'll scout ahead, after a quick breakfast."

When the time came, they jogged several miles toward the Spanish Peaks. Trinidad lay back to their southeast. Qualls knew the way between ridges in this hilly land north of the looming Ratons.

"Kid, I like your work," the man said after a long silence. "You never shirk, an' you speak up for work that takes special grit."

The Texan glanced away. This sudden directness took him aback. Here rode the man who only a few days before had balked at even taking him on the drive.

But Marks had grown up in the saddle. At ten he was made of rawhide and flint, a true son of his father. Now, by seventeen, he'd busted hard mustangs, worked ornery "mossy horn" steers out of their hideouts, been captured by Comanche raiders and escaped, been clawed by savage brush, sped over country ripped by "gully-washers" to get stampeding herds milling. He'd grown up paying attention to some of the Southwest's most adept teachers—his pa, brothers, and the brand of cow people by which they set store.

He'd smelled plenty of hair and hide under the heat of a branding iron, had the scent of sagebrush on his pants, and felt the pain of thirst between watering places.

Qualls had opposed his coming. But Qualls knew a humility that could turn once he saw he'd made a mistake. Marks pondered what had drawn out this comment by the foreman. He'd done just what other men did. The entire outfit, to a man, was top-notch in his book, every one of them true blue to the brand.

"Thanks," he replied. "Just hope I can pull my weight . . . get the herd through for those fine folk."

Qualls chuckled. They rode on. The first pinkish

glory of morning tinged the eastern horizon. About them was the fresh scent of piñon, sage, juniper, and mesquite. Along some of the many water courses that slashed out of higher country they saw dark lines of cottonwoods that liked to hug the water. They also knew there were willows, chokeberries, and wild plums. Here and there scrub oak appeared.

"You remind me of somebody." It was the boss again. He let his horse jog on a ways before he took it up again. Marks waited, letting vigilant eyes sweep the landscape as he noted what Qualls was doing. "Had me a wife and a son . . . Bud. We lived on a little spread. The wife, she was the joy of my eyes. The son, I figgered he was goin' to be a man to be proud of. Grew to be sixteen . . . almost your age. One afternoon, I headed for home after checkin' some cattle at the far side of my range. Came over a hill, then I saw it. Smoke! House an' barn goin' up, an' me five minutes away at a dead run."

He couldn't continue. It was a half-minute before he got his voice back. "When I came flyin' in, first one I looked for was Bertie, my wife. Bertie was lyin' where a cottonwood roof pole crashed down on her. She'd tried to pull some of our things out before the fire got 'em, things we'd worked hard for. Still alive. Whispered she was glad I'd come in time to say good-bye. She told me again she loved me . . . said I'd been good to her an' Bud. Gasped out who did it, a big rancher greedy to hog the range and drive us out. Then she said, 'Bart, you'd be proud of our son. He never wanted to hurt anybody, was so gentle, but he stood up to those men, got two of 'em for keeps. Fought like you'd a fought, Bart. Then he chased the rest off. Go find Bud, Bart.' Then Bertie died in my arms after I'd dragged her free, away from the fire."

Again the trail boss gazed away. Grief had made his voice very labored.

Marks waited a long time. "What about Bud?" he finally asked.

"I found him. It was out along the back trail the burnin' bunch had taken. He'd stayed with 'em a short distance . . . till he took a bullet. He fell from his horse, but I could read from his tracks he'd staggered a ways back, tryin' to get to his ma. He had died 'fore I reached 'im. Just that mornin' he'd told me, 'Pa, I like ridin' with you. I want always to ride with you.' But I told him to stay home that day. How'd I know it would end that very day?

"Well, I buried Bertie an' Bud. Put up crosses with their names, put flowers from the hill on their graves. Then I went lookin'. Knew just where I'd find the men that did it. They'd gone to this little settlement to celebrate. They had more range, they thought. When they saw me ride in to confront 'em, the boss an' one of his men started shootin'. They kept closin' in on me, yellin' they meant to finish the job. I shot back, an' when I rode out they both lay dead. I never wanted to stop 'em like that. Thought I might reason with 'em, get 'em to see the grief they'd caused by their greed. But they forced it. A third man rode to see me later an' left his gun at home. He apologized. Said he'd never dreamed when the boss an' the other man led him and two others to our place things would go as far as they did. Helped me build a cabin and put up a barn."

"But you didn't stay there," Marks said.

"No. Sold the place, took the driftin' fever. I felt so lonely without Bertie an' Bud I just rode for days. Then I met Frank Spellman in Texas. He was takin' a herd to Abilene, and hired me. Frank asked me to ramrod his new ranch, but I stayed in Abilene, workin' in the stockyards. He rode on back to join his wife an' daughter. A few days later, I realized I should've gone with 'im. So I headed along the Santa Fe Trail with a wagon train bound for Santa Fe. Here I am. Shoot, kid, I've talked your ears off."

"Glad you told me."

"Yeah. Man feels free gettin' it off his chest. A lot of times I rummage back to the days with Bertie an' Bud. When you throwed down on that man Ike that meant to murder me, I said, 'Qualls, that's the kind of thing Bud would've done for you if he could.' An' when I thought some more about you yearnin' to ride on this drive, I said, 'Yeah, Qualls, that's what Bud would've asked for.' Thing that matters is a man's a man. The question is not whether he's seventeen or thirty. A young man needs a chance to show what he can do—to bring out the good if he's got it in him."

"You know," Marks returned, "you remind me a lot of Pa. The way you handled those men plottin' to rustle made me chuckle."

They pushed on. The paleness of very early morning brightened as the sun fully rose. Presently they came on tracks of unshod Indian ponies. Marks dismounted to examine the tracks closely.

"Twelve ponies," he concluded after searching the area. "Cut through goin' west not more than an hour or two ago."

Qualls was pleased at the rider's timing of the tracks. "And how do you know the time *that* close?" he inquired.

"Easy," said Marks. "You see these older tracks over here, left by a deer. Made before this silvery insect trail laid during the night. The Indian pony tracks don't have any insect sign. They're too recent. Another thing: See this wild turkey track under the pony prints? That turkey came off its night roost in a tree," he pointed to a line of trees along a creek to the north a short stone throw. "He wouldn't have gotten down before an hour or two ago at the earliest."

Qualls nodded. They followed the pony tracks a ways. The Indians had kept their mounts to a doggedly straight course where terrain allowed, striking for the mountains.

"I see, too, that they're movin' at a steady jog." Qualls could read this sign by the spacing and sharpness of the hoof prints. "They'll find good huntin' in the foothills an' on up.

"One of the chiefs that's been causin' grief among the settlers in the territory is Coronaldo. His bunch is vicious . . . often leave some dead. They almost always get away with cattle as well as horses. They've struck some army supply wagons, too, an' were after rifles as well as food."

He explained that he'd learned this from the man running the stagecoach stop in the patched ruins of Bent's old fort on the Arkansas. He'd heard more at Trinidad, and from Lucien Maxwell and Uncle Dick Wootton.

"I reckon they'd put lusty eyes on the beef we're trailin'," replied Marks. "Twelve of 'em. They, plus others they might pick up, could give us a rugged fight."

"An' they know the country like you know the back of yore hand. When these tribes run off cattle, those who follow don't get 'em back often." Qualls shook his

114

head. "I shore don't want to lose this herd, or any of 'em."

The ramrod said he knew some of the way through the rolling plain. He hoped to stay clear of bad traps if Indians lurked in wait.

"But there's one place we'll reach in about three days. They could pounce on us sudden, whittle our number fast. It's at a canyon leadin' into a good waterin' place in a grassy basin. The canyon has steep walls an' some rock fortresses along the rims, with plenty of brush an' trees. The herd will need the water. But we need to come up with a way to stop any Indians that may plan to hit us there."

Less than a half hour later, the two riders split up to look for water for the middle of the day or evening. Marks found a couple of basins that held plenty of water. Climbing into a tall scramble of boulders skirting one of these, he let his gaze comb the area around and ahead for a few miles. The water gleamed like silver in the morning sun.

Satisfied that he was quite alone, he remembered. Going to his horse, he reached into a saddlebag. At long last, here was a chance to open the sack and see the surprise.

The sack was heavy. He got the rawhide thong loose and peered inside. Then he felt his mouth watering. Candy of various kinds—peanut brittle, taffy, molasses chips. He whistled in a sweet-toother's ecstasy. It had been a long time since he'd had a haul like this!

"Ah, Mrs. Spellman! Jackie! You know my weakness!" He drew out some peanut brittle and tried it. "Wahooooeeeeee!" As he crunched on the deliciousness, he imagined the ladies laughing at his delight.

That was when he felt it. Along the sides of the sack, falling almost into his fingers, was an envelope. Mystified, he pulled it out. His name was on the front. Sliding a nail along the seal, he brought the contents out quickly. It was a note from Jackie. Also there was another, smaller envelope, sealed, with the name "Smiley" on it. The handwriting on the "Smiley" envelope was different from Jackie's.

First he unfolded Jackie's note to him. The note read:

Dear Marks,

We are grateful for what your brother Lonan did for us, and for what you are doing now. I'll pray that, whatever happens, you'll be safe. Ma and I love the music box. It means so much to us, as it gets lonely sometimes. Josh and I will be married soon, and the days until then seem slow to both of us. I do hope you'll be back for the wedding. I'll be so glad. Enjoy the surprise from Ma and me.

Voni Scovil left the other envelope with me for Smiley. She said she did not want her uncle to be aware of it. He must not approve of her friendship with Smiley. I am not sure why, but he seems to watch her almost every moment. I know you'll be sure that Smiley gets her message when it can be kept secret. It must be very special.

My gratitude and earnest prayers.
Jackie Spellman

Marks gazed off into the broad distances of the Colorado Territory to the north toward the Arkansas. A faint smile played beneath the broad brim that shielded him from the sun. "Thanks, Mrs. Spellman. Thanks, Jackie." He crunched on more of the sweets. "And Voni, I hope what you say to Smiley makes him as happy as I'd like for him to be."

He spotted Qualls far off on a hill. The boss was waving his hat for him to join him going back the way they had come. So, back to the herd.

Heading out, he remembered the canyon and basin that Qualls had described that morning. It surely sounded like that canyon might be an ideal place for Coronaldo or others to plot an ambush. Even if they did not, Qualls was wise in thinking ahead, being ready for the possibilities his shrewd mind told him. If they did try to grab the herd and destroy the drovers, what would the outcome be?

10

Ten bone-weary men rode with disgruntled spirits to an adobe northeast of Trinidad. It was tucked away beyond the shoulder of a ridge not far northwest from the Purgatoire River where it passed the buildings of Jim Gray's old ranch on the Santa Fe Trail from the Arkansas.

Fang Gatril breathed a sigh of relief. They had slunk through Ute-infested country safely under the cover of morning darkness to the herd's bedding ground. Then they had clung to the concealment of trees and brush, weaving their way here. Without their rifles for long-range fighting, they had summoned every caution to make it through without losing their scalps. Gatril seethed with hatred for the trail drovers. So they figured they had whipped Gatril and the men who rode with him! They'd see. And his mind weaved very special plans for Qualls.

"*Someone's* at the 'dobe," the squat Donk Bodeen hissed. He jerked a finger up the slope as he peered past piñons and junipers. They saw a small rectangle of light in a doorway. "May be Scovil, may not be. What do we do?"

"We ride in," growled Gatril. He was goaded by

gnawing hunger pangs and a craving for sleep. He'd prefer having a roof over his head. He twisted to others jogging nearby and threw up a hand that produced a halt. "Hacker! You an' Tyson git on up there. Find out fer sure who's there. If'n it's Scovil an' the other two, fine an' dandy. But if'n it's someone else, git rid o''em. I don't care how."

The two riders raked spurs to their mounts and sent them lunging up the incline the last quarter of a mile. A short time later they stood by the door and waved the rest of their outfit on up.

Gatril and the others came with the grunt of horses, creak of leather, and clink of bridle bits. Scovil stepped from the doorway. A stride behind him came Tontam. The second man swaggered as usual. A flicker of contempt danced in his eyes as he set his gaze on Gatril.

"What are you *all* doin' back here?" Scovil demanded. He moved out farther into the yard, his hand on his revolver butt. He was keeping his voice down. "You're supposed to be stayin' close to the herd, keepin' track of it. Only a messenger was to report."

"Yeah," Gatril scowled. Weariness and resentment were heavy in his voice. "Didn't pan out that way. Gart's dead, an' we ain't got our rifles. Can't go on in Injun country without rifles."

"Gart's . . . *dead?*" Scovil's tone was disbelieving, but it betrayed irritation too. He searched the eyes of the mounted man, anger flaming into his own face. His whole body had stiffened, and it was obvious he would be hard to deal with. "You don't have your rifles? With Indians and Coe's men around? What are you talkin' about?"

Gatril sighed and swung slowly down, biting a lip.

He cleared a dry throat. "Uh, Gart, he sneaked up on the herd. Got hisself bit by a rattler. Made it back in his saddle, straped on by the men handlin' the herd."

He elaborated briefly, then added: "He must've been so terrified the Spellman outfit heard 'im. They follered 'im right to our camp, an' had us dead to rights 'fore we knew they was all around. Rifles were thick as porcupine quills. Took our rifles, pistols, an' horses. We had to hoof it a couple o' hours to get the horses an' pistols. They hung on to our rifles, so we need more."

"Well, if that don't beat all!" Scovil spat in angry disgust. He shook his head to defame the riders. His eyes scorched Gatril's face, making the man feel lower than a snake's belly. "Let 'em sneak right up. An' you're supposed to know what you're doin'. Whatta you think I'm payin' you for—idiotic bunglin'?"

Scovil wheeled, paced a small, agitated circle, and kicked up dust. Finally he came back to Gatril. "All right. So you need rifles. We'll get some in Trinidad, some in the Plaza de los Leones, some at Francisco Plaza. But some o' you men who are not known will go for 'em. An' you'll be careful—*real* careful—not to do any talkin'. Go separately. Don't bunch the purchases, and don't cause anyone to wonder what you're up to. One other thing. The girl's inside. All of you, keep your paws off her. You hear me?"

He knew the low scum he hired to do his dirty work. The code of respect that most men of the West honored toward good women had long since been trampled under their feet.

Scovil turned back and stomped into the adobe. Voni, slumped at a rough table made of split cottonwood, held her face in her hands. She stared bleakly at a cup of coffee. Fear and dread clouded her bloodshot eyes.

"Got ten more mouths to feed, girl. They could devour a buffalo. Slap some breakfast together."

She pulled herself up slowly, shoved coal black hair from pale cheeks, and dragged herself about the room to prepare food. The meal consisted of two pans of fresh biscuits, a huge slab of salted pork, several "air-tights" of beans, and coffee made from grounds already in the pot.

As the girl worked, she kept rubbing her wrists. She glanced and winced at the iron clamps lying in a corner, fastened to a heavy chain. These had held her fast for many hours as she lay upon the dirty buffalo-hide bunk. Uncle Hu had left her there, with food within reach.

She felt the pain in her wrists. But another thing hurt too. She always was aware of Tontam gazing, could feel it even when her back was turned. Always he was looking, smirking in his taunting way when her eyes met his, like a wolf drooling over a lamb.

Scovil had laid down the law to the gunslinger again that morning, shortly before the others rode up. "I told you, an' I'm sayin' it again. Keep away from her till we've finished this." The words were terrifying: "Till we've finished this." What then? She shuddered. To be left to Tontam would be worse than death.

Hawk Mangis slouched over and reached impatiently for the coffeepot. He poured into a tin cup, tested the liquid with a finger, and sputtered under his breath. Not hot enough yet.

He set the pot back with a bang on the red-hot stove lid. Turning, he paused and laid a wolfish grin on Voni. She trembled and shrunk back. Then he laid his fingers on her woolen sleeve and let them slide down her arm. She jerked away and spun toward him, jabbing the

122

heated stove poker into his stomach. The heat seared through his shirt quickly, and he sprang back, erupting in a yelp of pain.

Tontam was right there. He rammed the barrel of his pistol brutally into Mangis's side like the blow of a hammer. Mangis howled in agony again, and the gunman flung him toward the door. "So you had to try it, did you? Now, git—git clean out!"

"Ah, no, no! I ain't done nothin'. Jest funnin'." Mangis caught himself from falling at the door, then Tontam raised a boot and planted it on his rump, ramming him past the banging door. Mangis fell into the yard, plunging to his knees in the dust.

"Now, git up! Fill yore hand!"

Mangis started to pick himself up. He gazed at the gunman in disbelief. His face was a torture of wild fear. He was whining, rubbing dust from trembling hands on greasy pants. "I ain't no match for you with a gun. It's crazy."

"Huh! If yo're too yeller-livered to draw," Tontam sneered, "then remember! Remember good! Don't you ever, ever touch her again!"

Mangis stood up, felt his stomach and his side, smarting from pain. "Yeah . . . shore," he mumbled. He'd lived by the gun when he had the drop, but he knew when he was up against a black deuce. Tontam was far and away too fast. Relief at Tontam letting him off stole across his face, flushing away the sickening fear.

"An' you can eat out here," Tontam fired another shot. He whirled to face the others. They had poured from the adobe or edged near from places in the yard. All were gaping at him. "Anyone got an argument? Spit it out now. An' go fer yore gun when you say it." Tontam leered mockingly at the faces. He studied each visage. No takers. He snorted contempt as if he were a winning longhorn bull and stalked back inside.

Mangis slapped dust from his knees, blinked sheepishly, and walked nervously about the yard. He muttered sulkily under his breath. Gatril's face was a black scowl. He crouched near the door that was still open and nervous fingers spun up a cigarette. The day of the peacock was short, he consoled himself.

After breakfast, Scovil walked from the adobe with the men. Mangis was in the yard as Tontam had decreed. Scovil spread out a map and laid it on a large rock.

"I've spent a lot of time going over this area," the boss said. "I've spent days in it, studied it like them scholar dudes pore over the lines of Shakespeare. Paid old Braid Mallas to guide me. He knew the area south of the Arkansas better than most—every hill, every canyon, every creek. He showed me how to stay out of sight from Zan Hicklin at his Greenhorn Ranch, away from the stage stations at the San Carlos and at Muddy Creek, an' avoid bein' seen by Peter Dotson or his Mexican sharecroppers over here near the Wet Mountains. There are trails that will keep us clear of the villages like the Plaza de los Leones, here, an' Fort Francisco or Francisco Plaza, here.

"You go this way, you see. Gatril, you've got the copy I gave you. I want you all to learn the lay of the land, especially east an' southeast of the Wet Mountains—here, see? There's a winding route to push the herd west, get past Dotson's ranch near where the San Carlos spills out of the rocks, an' find the narrow trail between steep ridges into a hidden valley. It's marked with an X.

"Pay attention to the whole area around here, as if

your lives depended on it, for well they might. Know how to work a herd up to the pass into the valley even in the black of night. The trail in from the east, through a gorge slicing northwest, is just a horse trail, though I hear Dotson plans to blast out a wagon road. Cattle can make it as you let 'em string out an' file in.

"Plenty of grass an' water in the valley. Here's where you camp, at this run-down adobe. You'll be in a basin that drops down like a huge hole, where Rebel recruits camped while Union soldiers hunted for them. We can hold cattle in the hole till every drover has given up or is dead. If any hang around, we can bushwhack 'em one by one, get shed of the bodies, hide the horses.

"We'll ride on a day or so together. Then Tontam an' the girl an' I will split off. I plan to visit the herd. That won't raise any suspicions. I'm just a man checkin' on his investment, see. I'll pick up all the information I can. Where they plan to bed down an' what their strategy is for the nights after they pass the Huerfano Butte, here, an' approach the area southeast an' east of the pass into 'Mace's Hole.'

"You'll explore this area by night, not bein' seen, but otherwise lay up in the valley. When we see you after visitin' the herd, we'll know more. Then we'll make our final plans for the big move."

Jawbone, driving the chuck wagon ahead of the herd in the late afternoon, saw Smoky Dobis. The black cowboy was circling in from a jaunt farther ahead. Jawbone gathered some driftwood near the trail. He tossed it into the cowhide cuna sling stretched under the wagon bed between the axles to carry wood and buffalo chips for fires.

"You said Bart gave you leave to hunt a deer," Jawbone called when the rider got near enough. He settled on the wagon seat and took up the reins. "Spotted ary a one yet?"

"Nary," replied the cowhand. He ran fingers through his kinky hair, freed of his sweaty hat for a moment. "But soonah or latah I'se gwinna fetch one in. Nevah yo mind."

Jawbone slapped the team into motion and nodded farewell to the black drover, a good friend of Bose Ikard, who was a black cowboy riding with Charley Goodnight. "Fine men, the both of 'em," the cook mused as the wagon rumbled northward.

Smoky watched the serpentlike line of the herd winding toward him off a distant hill. He loped on ahead of Jawbone again to swing in another great loop. He figured he could flush a deer out of a draw, and they'd have venison for supper. About a mile ahead of Jawbone, he spotted a fat buck bounding off through brush toward a ridge to the northwest. Spurring his mount and lifting his Henry rifle, he gave chase.

Unable to get a clear shot at the game due to brush and small ravines, Smoky waited for a mile or so. He was patient for a better crack at the animal. This came as he rounded the shoulder of the ridge to the west, out of Jawbone's sight. Throwing his rifle up for shot, he was about to press the trigger. At that second the buck, spooked by something up on the hillside, cut sharply back to the north down the incline.

It was then that Smoky saw the horses. His eyes, flitting over the terrain for a further chance, fell on the two mounts. They stood in the shade of a huge rock outcropping about a quarter of a mile away. He lowered the Henry to his saddle bow. Suddenly he was wary.

The buck bounded into a stand of brush and vanished. Smoky started to work his way, undetected, toward the horses. He needed a view closer up which he might report to Qualls.

Then he saw two people, a man and a woman. They stood beside another large rock. Smoky dropped into a buffalo wallow and let his horse climb out of it where he could see again. The woman's back was turned toward Smoky. He had no idea who she was. The man appeared to be doing something to the woman's arms. The cowboy shucked a pair of field glasses he'd picked up at the scene of a skirmish between the U.S. Cavalry and Comanches along the Pecos. Laying probing scrutiny on the two people, he noted that the woman had half-turned. He whistled very low as he concentrated on the arms. Wrist irons! The woman was a prisoner!

"Sho 'nuff," he muttered to his horse. Mystified, he played the glasses on the man's face. That jolted him with surprise. "Why, dat's Scovil!" He shifted the focus of the glasses to the second person. "Ah. Dat's his niece. But why dem irons? Lawdy hab mercy! Mistah Qualls will sho 'nuff wanta know 'bout dis."

Smoky pushed the glasses back into his saddlebag. He started to take up his reins from their dally around the horn. A slight rattle of a dislodged stone behind him made him spin. Instinctively, he grabbed for his rifle across the pommel.

"Why the irons?" The voice was challenging. The smile was the wicked gleam of a wolf that has a calf backed against a high bank with no way out. The gunman Tontam! He held a six-shooter, the winning hand.

"Ah, it's you Mistah Tontam. I'se wid da herd—da herd Mistah Scovil is havin' us drive." Smoky hoped he might relax now. Strange as the sight he'd witnessed, these were not part of the Gatril rustling bunch after all. The gunman would slide that gun into its holster.

"With the herd," Tontam drawled. "An it 'pears you saw too much fer yore own good."

"What's dat? Whatta you mean?" Smoky had caught the tone and especially the gunman's choice of words. He flung a glance back toward Scovil and the girl. Suddenly the two were nowhere in view. Only their two horses still stood where he had seen them.

"I mean," said the cold steel voice, "yore string has run out. You cash in yore chips here."

Fear clutched at Smoky's chest as if talons had dug into his flesh. He felt a chilling sickness drop into his stomach. A shot behind this ridge would never be heard back there where Jawbone rolled along.

"You'se gotta be bluffin' me." His throat felt as dry as cotton on the plantation where he'd dragged his long sack. His words came hardly above a whisper.

"No bluffin'." Tontam grinned. The relish of a hungry lobo shone in his eyes. He reached cautiously and took away Smoky's rifle, his pistol hand poised for an instant shot. "Now, unbuckle the gun belt an' hand it down careful."

Working at this nervously, Smoky wondered about his bowie knife. It rested in its scabbard on his belt. He also considered the thin chance of making it if he drove spurs to his horse. He could whip his body to the far side, and tear out of there.

"Now, git off, an' lead yore horse back over here." The man wielding the gun nodded to his right on the hill. The brush was higher there. It could conceal a horse and help cover a death shot.

Smoky eased his boot nearest Tontam free of its stirrup. He shifted as if to dismount.

In a blur of speed his right hand flung his hat at Tontam's face. At the same instant Smoky whipped his body low to the far side, trying to put the horse between him and the murderer. His left hand gripped the saddle horn and his right streaked to the cantle for another clutch.

The horse bolted forward as Smoky yelled. Tontam dropped the rifle and gun belt from his left hand. He took a step forward and fired. His first bullet hit Smoky high in the right leg as it swung over the horse's rump. As the cowboy's mount lunged forward, two more shots barked on the ridge. One of the bullets struck Smoky in the shoulder as he tried to duck low. He tumbled into the dust and low brush, tried to spring up, and took the third bullet high in his side.

The horse tore on, panicked, circling to the brush down the slope. His head was thrown high so that the reins did not drag, and the stirrups slapped wildly. Smoky pitched over across a juniper. He was dead by the time he came to a still heap.

The gunman poked his gun into the cowboy's ribs and checked his work. Death was sure. Searching in a saddlebag, he drew out what he sought—a broken arrow about a foot long. The flint head was intact. Trapping Smoky's horse against a sand bank, he rammed the arrowhead very hard into the saddle leather. It stuck.

That done, Tontam turned the horse loose. Going back, he brushed out tracks his own boots had made. He dragged Smoky's body to a nest of rocks and quickly but carefully covered it, along with the man's rifle and gun belt. Scanning the hillside, he brushed out more tracks and signs of the action.

He had moved fast. When he rejoined Scovil and Voni, the girl looked at him questioningly.

"You shot the Indian?" Scovil asked, winking slyly.

"Yeah." Tontam's face was a smirk, hidden by his hat brim as he dried his face with a bandana, "He was lyin' over there watchin' the herd. Well, he won't be goin' back to tell the other braves."

"Come on, then," Scovil urged. "We'll ride on a ways. Later, we'll ride in after they've camped an' we won't be in the way."

Voni pulled herself wearily into her saddle. They turned their horses down the slope to the north. But the question she had about Tontam's shots lingered.

11

Jawbone yanked the team to a stop, set the brake, and clambered down from his seat. He stood with hands on hips, waiting for the trail boss and his young companion to rein in from their ride. Now they were coming in from the northeast a half hour before sundown.

"I can't figger Smoky," were the cook's first words.

"Smoky? What about him?" Qualls queried, swinging down to stomp about and stretch. He felt a weariness from being in the saddle for hours.

"He taken off nigh on three hours back," explained the cook. He scratched his chin. "Said he'd fetch me in a deer. He ain't even showed hisself. Ain't like Smoky."

In a land where Indians had been especially hostile the past few years, a man could easily think of the worst.

"Where'd you see him last?" Marks inquired.

"That hill off to the right o' the wagon a few miles back." They remembered it. "Smoky headed toward it on the east, an' taken out like he'd spotted a deer. Then he passed out of my sight."

"We'll find him," Qualls assured, looping up his reins and climbing back into leather. "May be trouble, may not. I'll stop the herd off yonder in that flatland where they can graze an' water from the crick. There isn't much water, though, an' we'll trail 'em farther tonight or very early tomorrow to better water, dependin' on what we find."

Jawbone swung the chuck wagon out near the creek by some cottonwoods and willows, pointed its tongue toward the north, and camped. The two riders headed in opposite swings around the approaching cattle to see if they could spot Smoky or find any drover who had caught sight of him. When they reached a rendezvous back of the drag, they exchanged nods that left them grim.

"All right," said Qualls, "we'll pick up Wile an' Shag, then all of us will fan out over the back trail. We may have bad trouble. So keep within gunshot sound. Be ready for anything, an' if you hit danger, give us a couple of shots an' we'll burn the wind to get there."

The four rode at a lope. A little below a half hour later, Wile waved his hat to Marks afar off, who joined him a short way east of the hill Jawbone had mentioned. Wile had come across Smoky's horse.

" 'Pears real bad," Wile yelled. He swung the lost rider's horse around, and Marks saw the arrow. Grimly they examined it.

"Something doesn't make sense," Marks said. "If an Indian shot Smoky, why would he leave a good horse an' all this saddle leather behind?"

"Maybe Smoky came on one, two, or more of 'em an' ran 'em off," Wile Gaster ventured hopefully. "He might be laid up somers waitin' for us."

"If so, we need to find him fast." They mounted, and Wile led the riderless horse, climbing in a loop around the ridge. Marks spoke again. "Odd the arrow would be snapped off like that. Any tree or brush that would break off an arrow that strong would jerk the arrowhead in the leather, forcing it back. Yet the arrow was sticking straight in. The brush around here isn't that tall. An' did you notice the end of the arrow where it was snapped off? It wasn't broke fresh, not today. It shows time—maybe weeks or months since it was broke."

Gaster halted his horse. His enormous body twisted in the saddle, and he whistled in awe. "You noticed all them things, that fast? Yo're a good man—like yore brother Lonan." He pulled out his pistol. "You know the signal Qualls told us, two shots." He fired the shots into the air, waiting for Smoky or the other two searchers to respond. Two shots sounded, and in a short time Qualls and Shag pounded around the hill.

The four began a methodical hunt. They spread out around the hill as the sun plunged its fiery tip halfway behind the peaks in the west.

Shag yelled from the slope on the north. Marks, closest to him, galloped his horse over for a look-see. Shag had come on an area of loose dirt churned up, probably by horse hooves. It exposed fresher dirt than the area around it, blown by wind after a light rain. Marks got down and soon noted that someone had tried to brush out tracks. Here and there he detected the curved lines where a hat had swept over the ground. He also saw, just as Shag pointed, that a young juniper had been squashed down by some impact.

"Here," Marks invited. "Spots where the toes of his boots dug in. Maybe it was when he fell or rolled." Beneath the juniper plant and out of view unless a man searched closely, he found an imprint from a man's fingers.

Marks fired two more shots into the air to summon Qualls and Gaster.

They began a probing scrutiny of the area. A minute or so after, Marks discovered the imprint of a man's boot. It was driven deeply into the soft dirt about ten paces from the juniper, up the slope toward a nest of rocks. No doubt it had missed the eye of the person who had brushed out the tracks, for it was gouged into a mat of grass over soft dirt and had not shown up like the nearby tracks.

Now that he'd come onto something, Marks discovered other telltale signs approaching the rocks higher up. There was a small hole where a stone had been kicked loose, a splotch of blood on the twig of a scrubby bush. Then he spotted another splotch of blood hidden in a patch of grama. Half a minute later Qualls found a small strip of caked mud mingled with grass. No doubt the mud had clung to a man's boot heel at a water hole or creek a few hours back. Farther up, Marks pointed to a small, broken branch from a low sage bush, ground into a flat rock beneath it. Shag nodded.

"Movin' toward those rocks," Marks surmised.

They scrambled up among boulders and rocks. The lure of discovery spurred them to greater haste. But dread of what they would find hung like a pall over the ridge.

"Blood," Marks announced. He jabbed a finger toward a crimson streak along the side of a boulder. It was out of sight from a person standing and gazing about to cover up any signs of a foul deed. "More over here." He began to throw rocks aside, but he was trembling at what he might uncover.

They saw a sleeve and the dark-skinned back of a

hand. A sickening feeling clutched at their stomachs, for they knew it had to be Smoky. Going on with the difficult task, they uncovered the face.

"Ah, Smoky!" Shag exclaimed, and drew off his hat, his shoulders slumping in dejection.

They lifted their friend out and toted his body down where they could lay it gently on the ground.

Further search turned up other clues. "A boot gouged up dirt here," Marks said. He found a faint trail down the slope. A few minutes later he came to the spot where a man had caught a horse against a bank. He pursued the horse tracks back to where Smoky, apparently, had tumbled into the young juniper.

"Up here," Qualls called. He had found the piñon where a horse, probably the killer's, had waited. The men looked at the stomped-up ground, but Marks searched the tree. He noticed that the animal had rubbed its neck on a sturdy branch, probably due to an itch. On the branch he found the flake of a scab mixed with blood. Attached to it was a bit of hair.

The horse had a sore on its neck. And from the angle the horse had stood, probably the sore was on the left side. Examining the hair, the young rider could tell that it was the color of a mouse. Mexicans dubbed it a *grulla*, their word for a crane of a mousy gray color that inhabited some of the marshy regions in the Southwest.

Once he was sure, Marks told the others what he'd found.

"Marks, I get more amazed the longer I watch you work," said Qualls. "You don't miss a trick. I've heard men talk about Charley Goodnight an' some others havin' unusual skills in observing. You seem to be of the same breed."

"I'm learning," Marks admitted. "They say Goodnight spent a lot of time an' effort developing his ability, observing birds, animals, and other things even as a boy. So've I. Observing little things that most men pass over has saved my life a few times. Pa taught all us boys to tell the colors of horses we were trailing even before we'd seen them."

"Yeah, by the hair a bush might grab," spoke up Gaster.

"That," replied Marks, "and a few other things. Stick with them till the men stop for camp and strip off the saddles. You know how the horses like to roll. You find their hairs in the grass or dust. Look around awhile and you find several colors."

"Well, now," said the ramrod, "I know what you'll look for next. Simple. You'll want to see where the grulla taken off to."

"Yeah."

Gaster, a huge man, laid the body of his dead friend across his saddle for his final ride. He worked some diamond hitches to secure him. The others searched for the grulla's tracks on the rocky and sandy ridge. Dusk was laying its graying light across the land, but they found that the tracks went to join two other horses. Then the three sets of tracks led on northward, plunging into a deep ravine that snaked north and northwest. But Marks did not find any more hair to give away the colors of the other two mounts, and on rocky ground he could not pick up any clues from boot tracks.

It had become too dark to follow without dismounting and bending down often to scan the ground in the light of matches. At several points, the horses might have left the ravine.

"Come mornin'," said Qualls, "we'll ride back, take a better, longer look."

As they struck out toward the chuck wagon and the herd, Marks mused aloud. "It's interesting. The man that did Smoky in wanted us to think Smoky ran into Indian arrows. He didn't reckon on us uncovering the body and learning that bullets killed him. And he didn't figure we'd find out he rides a grulla, a grulla with a sore on its left neck. Or that he has two other people with him. And another thing is, he left Smoky's rifle and pistol buried in the rocks with Smoky. Indians would value those guns. And Indians wouldn't bother to bury Smoky or leave his horse."

"Yeah," Qualls took it up, "but he didn't hanker to be caught with the guns. An' he didn't kill for the horse, the saddle, or the canteen. Even the money's still in Smoky's pocket, most o' the last thirty he was paid. We've covered a lot of the main motives for murder. Why did he kill Smoky?"

"The reasons go on and on," Marks rejoined. "Some do it for the cussedness. Or suppose the killer's someone Smoky recognized?"

"May be somethin' to that," Gaster chipped in. "Could've been a hombre that didn't want to be seen out here."

The camp was dejected after they rode in and explained. Jawbone dragged himself through the motions of getting supper. Smoky had been extremely well-liked, and surely must have been one of the finest of many faithful black cowboys who trailed herds or worked ranches.

Marks and Smiley took turns shoveling out a grave on a little knoll. The men laid Smoky to rest wrapped in his blanket and slicker. Smiley read from a well-worn American Bible Society Bible of 1859. Then he said a few things about the hope of a Christian, which brought tears to many an eye. Qualls added his comments, and said he believed in the Resurrection when trusting folk would have new bodies that never would die. Smiley prayed in a simple, sincere way. They filled in the lonely grave and put up a cross. Hap Bailey had whittled out crude letters for the name "Smoky Dobis" and the year 1867.

Qualls said he'd write to Smoky's hometown back in Georgia in hopes of notifying his relatives. He sat against a wheel of the wagon, scratching out a brief message.

The men had been hungry. But nobody seemed inclined to eat. Only the cattle ate their supper with relish. The men just sat around talking in low tones, with many lapses into silence. Finally, after a long time, Jaw-bone came around telling them in kindly words they ought to eat a bite. Smoky would want them to, he added. So they began to take tin plates and come to his pot for supper.

Marks, looking at Smiley, told him he liked his words beside the grave.

"Shore," the cowboy said, his voice still heavy with grief. "I meant every word, because I believe. It hurts, but I know this, because Smoky told me once, he's in a far better place tonight."

Marks thought of the letter he carried in his saddle-bag. The hours had been so packed he had seen no chance to deliver it to Smiley. He strode toward his saddle to produce it.

"Smiley," said Qualls, "you an' Hap finish supper pronto. Ride a wide circle around camp. Keep together an' within the sound of a rifle. Watch for anything that don't look right. Report back in a couple of hours, an' others will go out."

Marks heard the order and saw the sense of it. He pushed the envelope back into his pants pocket. Smiley had no chance now. He could not read in the darkness on his special patrol. And he knew better than to try to read it in the flare of a match out there. The letter would have to wait a few more hours.

The two horsemen faded into the darkness, leaving camp.

Maybe, Marks mused, the letter would have sweet words after a bitter day.

12

Those at the cow camp heard a yell. Riders were coming in. An instant later every man was on his feet moving to his saddled horse, rifle in hand. Qualls had instilled haste in them, and they kept fresh mounts ready for instant use at all times. They ate every meal with rifles at their sides.

Qualls led his own horse hastily away from the circle of light from the fire and waited. He'd heard a horse jogging closer from the northern end of the bedding ground. When the animal finally became recognizable out of the darkness, it turned out to be Pete Tallam's horse. The drover brought the mount to a halt when he made out his boss stalking toward him.

"Three riders, comin' in peaceful," he reported. "Chip passed on the word it was the man buyin' this herd, Scovil. Two others with 'im."

"Scovil? Huh! Well, he said he'd pay us a visit. Well, tell 'em to ride right on in. Three, eh? Is there a lady, too?"

"Chip said they was a woman." Pete grinned. "Me, I waren't close enough in the dark to tell a woman."

"Pete, I didn't know you needed light to tell a

woman," the ramrod chuckled. He needed a little lightness after the dark news of the day.

"Ah, shucks," Pete came back as he hauled his horse about to take the message, "I can tell one purty good. Only I ain't never been able to tell one nothin' that done any good." With that he spurred away.

The three riders came on, walking their horses. Qualls called out a greeting, and Scovil answered. Then the visitors swung into the glow of light and the boss walked with them closer to the fire.

"Wile," Qualls called, "take their horses, unsaddle 'em, feed 'em some oats, an' stake 'em out to graze with the others near the wagon. See they get water from the crick, too. Get down, folks. Yo're probably starvin' for a bite. Jawbone's grub is good, the best this side o' the Muddy Creek Station stage stop. An' yo're welcome."

"Welcome words," Scovil grunted wearily as he stepped down. He turned to see his niece dismount. "We've come a far piece today—all the way from Trinidad. Laid up for a while near the Spanish Peak on the east when we spotted Injuns 'fore they saw us. Then we swung a bit east, an' missed you. Later, we guessed we'd passed you, so we rode back a ways."

Jawbone shook out a pair of blankets for the two men to sit on. He set down a wooden grocery box on which Voni could sit comfortably. "Supper's waitin'," he announced. "Hop to it an' fill up yore plates."

Voni went first, then the other guests. After them, Qualls and the riders free from herd duty at the moment filed over to the coffee again. Marks hunkered down near Voni. He noted that she sagged as if she were extremely tired.

"Not all of us are here," he told her. "Hap an' Smiley

were sent out for a couple of hours to scout for signs of trouble."

She nodded. Disappointment registered on her face, which she was wiping with a wet cloth.

"Are you all doing well?" she asked.

"We've held the herd." Marks did not want to mention Smoky. That would be bad news for her at any time, especially right before she was to eat. Anyhow, Qualls could break that word in his own time. "With men like Qualls an' Smiley, the herd's in the best of hands."

"I—I keep believing that. And I've prayed a lot. How—how is Smiley?"

"Regular songbird," he said with a grin. "Best singin' cowboy a herd could drift off to sleep on. He's our favorite singer, Smiley is. One of the most respected men in the outfit."

That pleased her. She smiled despite the exhaustion that placed a strain on her pretty features. He started to mention the letter he'd wanted to pass on to Smiley. He needed to explain that he still hadn't gotten it into the cowboy's hands. But Tontam strode over, his plate piled, and sat down on the blanket close to her box. Marks decided he had better wait.

Qualls sat down next to Scovil, who was between the segundo and Tontam. "Wasn't really sure you'd drop in on us out here. Figgered maybe due to the hard ride you might stay at Zan Hicklin's place on Greenhorn Creek, as so many have the past few years, or go on to the Muddy Creek where the meals an' the beds are good. It's dangerous country for anyone, let alone havin' a lady along."

Scovil washed down a big bite full with a chaser of

hot coffee. "That we know," he responded. "But sometimes the stagecoaches are so bumpy. An' we wanted to show her some of the country better. We did have a nice place to stay at Trinidad."

Marks, watching Voni pick at her food despite the hunger that would be natural after such a day, noted something. The girl glanced at her uncle, bit her lip, then stared at her plate.

"I'm a bit anxious about the herd," Scovil went on. His eyes had shifted to Voni, then back to Qualls. "My brother Matt's countin' heavy on it. I like to keep a good account of our investments, so I wanted to see firsthand how you're doin' and what the prospects are."

"Shore, shore," Qualls acknowledged. He savored his coffee in meditative silence for a time. Marks noted that the ramrod had not yet mentioned the great heartache of the day.

"No run-ins with Injuns or any other problems?" the buyer wanted to know.

"Well, I can't say that," the foreman drawled. "Matter o' fact, we ran head-on into our biggest problem this afternoon. Lost one of our top hands. Murdered." A heavy silence followed.

"Injuns?" Tontam finally queried. A forkload of beans was poised halfway to his mouth.

"We did find an arrow stickin' in his saddle," Qualls replied.

"Uh-huh! Injuns, then." Tontam went on with his eating. Scovil was chewing slowly, staring at his plate. Voni had ceased trying to eat, and she sat very quietly, her eyes troubled in the soft glow of the fire.

"Strange," Qualls said. "His horse was left. Injuns,

you know, run off any good stock they can use. You know how they've gotten away with so many from Trinidad to Denver."

"Well," Tontam spoke up again, "maybe yore man wounded some Injuns, an' they had to leave in a hurry."

"No, no, that won't wash," Qualls returned. "If the Injuns were that bad wounded, they wouldn't bother with Smoky's body, either. But whoever killed him did no scalpin' or mutilation, an' still had time to carry the body."

"Ahhhhhh. Yuh mean took the body right along with 'em?"

"No, not that. Just toted it far enough to cover it under a pile o' rocks. An' Injuns don't bury whites. They leave 'em lie. They don't even bury their own. They fix 'em on scaffolds in trees, high up."

Tontam put down a load of beef he had been ready to shove into his mouth. His eyes glinted hard at Qualls. Scovil put down his fork, and wiped the heel of a fist across his mouth, troubled. "Then," said Tontam, "yuh came across the body o' yore man?"

"Yeah. Wasn't hard. The man that murdered Smoky made a saddlebag full o' mistakes."

"What kind o' mistakes?" Tontam had become totally absorbed in the exchange. He had forgotten all about bolting down more food.

"Well," replied the trail boss, "Marks here spotted most of 'em right off. What about it, Marks?"

"The arrow," the young drover began, "was broken off about halfway down. I could tell from the break that it had been broken off weeks ago, not today. Did you ever hear of an Indian shooting a broken arrow? So it looked like the man that shot Smoky down in cold blood jabbed the arrow into his saddle to throw the killin' off on the wrong ones.

"Another thing—the arrow was broken at a point that would stand a pretty hard pressure before it broke. The pressure ought to push the arrowhead to the side in the saddle leather. But this arrow was jabbed straight in, nice and neat, not very deep.

"After we saw that, we found the place the killer shot from, even the spot where Smoky fell from his horse."

He hesitated at that point, leaving out the detail about a mouse-colored horse with a sore on its neck. Tontam, they all were aware, rode a mouse-colored gray. He had come in on it a few minutes earlier.

"Huh! That's mighty interestin'." Scovil sounded baffled. After a moment he glanced at Marks. "Sounds as if nothin' escaped your notice. I've heard about Dunlees like that."

"So the killer didn't use an arrow. He used a gun," Tontam said. He had gone to toying with the food he'd been so wolfish about a short time before. "Did you come across any tracks?"

"Oh, yeah, a lot of 'em once we searched around," Marks replied. "The killer made efforts to brush 'em out, an' must've figured he had. But he did a sloppy, halfway job. I mean downright careless. An' that might get him hanged. I reckon he just never counted on us finding the exact place where it happened. So he got lazy and over-confident. Killers often do that. Lazy, or he didn't see the need. There were boot prints, even horse tracks he'd missed. We followed them a ways."

"Hmmm," Tontam said thoughtfully. He cleared his throat. "Those tracks . . . did they tell you anythin'?"

"Shore," threw in Qualls. "They told us a right smart."

"Like what?"

"Well, for one thing the direction. The tracks led off to the north an' northeast, the way we've been takin' the herd. Of course, the riders could have hung a circle—to throw us off."

"Riders', you say? You mean there's more than one?"

"Shore. Three of 'em," Qualls went on, and sloshed down the last of his coffee, whereupon Jawbone brought him more. The group was quiet. After a long minute, the ramrod stood up. "Plenty left," he said. "Help yourselves again."

"Me, I've had enough," Tontam said.

"I suppose, darkness comin' on an' all, you couldn't follow them tracks very far," Scovil said.

"That's right," Qualls said with a nod. "But come daylight, we'll be out there."

"It all sounds so strange," Scovil said. "Why would anyone gun down one of your riders?"

"Maybe," said Qualls, "he wanted to thin out our ranks. We've still got a lot of treacherous country to take the herd through—a country, from all I hear, that has for years felt the toll of Injuns an' outlaws, what with the likes of the Mexican Trujillo, the Mexican Juan Mace they talk about, let alone other bad ones like the killer Charlie Dodge of Pueblo, the Jim Reynolds gang up from Texas, the Espinosa murderers that Tom Tobin tracked an' killed in 1863, an' more. If they cut us down, they make it easier to hit us later, try to grab the herd. You know how that Ike feller tried to do me in back 'fore we started. 'Fore that, there was the cinch cut that could've cost Frank his life."

He went on to tell them of the bunch of men who had had designs on the herd when it bedded on a meadow.

"They may or may not have had some connection with the loose-knit gang that hit Fort Union a few weeks back, runnin' off stock," Qualls said. "The bunch they say belonged to a man named William Coe."

"Yeah. All of which means you've just got to be even more careful from now on," Scovil cautioned. He had gone to pacing back and forth, plainly agitated. Having drawn out a perfecto, he'd lighted it and was puffing away. "But you bein' the man Frank told me you are, you can handle things. So far you've done a very good job. An' with riders like Marks here, an' the others, I feel good about the herd.

"By the way, what's your plan for the next three or four days gettin' to the Arkansas River? Where do you aim to stop for grass an' water?"

"That," said Qualls, "depends a bit on what we learn follerin' the killer's tracks tomorrow. We'll have firmer plans then." He did not commit himself further, and when Scovil pursued the matter, the ramrod handled it very well.

Talk went on, and Marks took Voni's and his plates and eating hardware to Jawbone's washtub. He poured more coffee, downed it, then moved nonchalantly over to the chuck wagon and beyond it to the horses staked out on good grass. Curiosity goaded him to get a look at Tontam's grulla—especially the left side of the neck. He didn't trust the man, and that was one mouse-colored horse that had been in this country today. Once he'd had a look, he meant to drift on out into the brush and get out of sight, then study by match light the tracks of the three visitor's horses coming in from the north.

He glanced back at the circle around the fire. Everyone seemed intent on what was being said. Then he spoke soothingly to the grulla and moved up to the left side of the neck. Striking a match, having the chuck wagon between himself and those at the fire, he cupped it to hide the flare from the sleeping longhorns lest he arouse them. Up behind the jaw, beneath the dark mane, he saw a spot of bare flesh left raw from rubbing. It was about the size of a boot heel. He blew out the match and stood pondering. He knew it might be just a strange coincidence. Horses rubbed against trees, corral poles, hitch rails, rocks and the like. But there was a fairly small chance a man would find two different horses—both grullas—the same day in the very same part of the country with a sore on the left side of the neck.

Thoughts whirled through his mind. He wanted to nail the man who cut Smoky down in the prime of life and stop the man—or men—who posed a threat to the herd and to people who meant a lot to him.

The song of a night rider was wafted on the gentle breeze sweeping in from Greenhorn Peak off to the northwest and other mountains. He listened for a time. A good sound, he thought, but not as good as Smiley's voice soothing the cattle.

"Hey, what yuh doin' with my horse?"

The voice sliced the air between them. Marks spun to see the dark form of Tontam. The man had slipped up as quietly as a cougar near the rump of the grulla.

"I'm not botherin' your horse," he said softly, shrugging it off.

"Why the interest in *my* horse? Yo're a livin' wonder, kid, figgerin' out all those things today—*if* you figgered 'em right. Don't let it run to yore head. Don't go tryin' to make some connection with *me.*"

"You?" Marks took his hat off and let the breeze play through his hair. "What reason would I have to do that?"

"None—not any good reason at all. I was jest thinkin' how you make connections—like three riders an' there bein' three of us. Pure coincidence, kid. Don't mean a thing."

"Strange you should tell me this," Marks replied. "Nobody spoke of connections touching you. A man that knows he's clear and free doesn't have to worry about connections like that."

"Implyin' I'm worried? Kid, I don't cotton to the way yuh talk. Yuh got somethin' in yore craw, spit it out. Don't play no game of words with me. I can cram the game right back down yore throat."

Marks stepped away from the horse. He spoke calmly, seeking peace. "If anyone's playing a game of words with you, it isn't me."

"Yuh fool kid! Yuh can't talk big like that to me! Ain't nobody does that! I'm gonna hammer yuh down a notch." He unbuckled his gun belt quickly and looped it on the horn of his saddle lying a few feet away on the grass.

Marks bit his lip. Was there no way out? He was one of Spellman's trusted riders, and one of Qualls's. He didn't want to get into a fight and embarrass them, or a commotion and disturb the herd. Yet this man would not understand or accept any graceful effort to prevent a fight. Tontam, a beast who lived by his touchy feelings, always had something he had to prove. What weakness must lie behind that outward show of bravado! He was a turkey tom and he had to swell.

"I'm working for Qualls," he said slowly. "He wouldn't want a fight." He started to step around Tontam. It took more grit to turn down a fight than to take it up.

"Naw, naw," Tontam snarled, his voice as vicious as a cougar's. "Yuh don't chicken out o' this!"

Marks unhooked his own gun belt and stepped away to lay it gently into a mat of grass.

He caught the flash of Tontam's dark body. The gunman was swinging before giving his opponent a chance to get set. Marks leaped back very fast and felt the wind of the cruel fist as an uppercut blazed by his face. While Tontam's arm was raised to complete its arc, Marks put all his weight behind a right of his own that struck just below the rib cage. He heard the air whoosh out of the man. Tontam doubled up, backing away in pain.

Marks bored in as quickly as a cat and slammed Tontam with a left to the jaw. Then he came around with a right to the chest that dumped the gunslinger backwards into the grass.

Others had made Tontam's mistake. They had assumed that because Marks was younger he could not handle himself the way the big boys played the game. Tontam had learned in one hard, quick lesson. He drew the heel of his hand across a mouth that spurted blood and hissed a curse. He fetched himself slowly to his feet, maddened to destroy.

Qualls and the others rushed over. The thud of fists on flesh had sounded loudly on the night air.

"Hey! What's this all about?" the ramrod thundered. "Break it up!"

Marks dropped his fists. He'd already gotten the

better of Tontam, and anyway, he had not wanted to fight. Tontam had forced it. And Marks respected his foreman.

"No! We don't break it up!" Tontam raged. He charged with the ferocity of a range bull. Now that others were watching, his vanity aroused him to look good. He drove a sweeping right at Marks's chin and Marks ducked under it. Then Marks got both feet under him, put all his hardened strength into it, and brought his two fists up into the attacker's stomach. Tontam was hauled off his feet, and as he sagged back down the Texan smashed him in the jaw with a fist of granite. Tontam was jarred sideways, and Marks hammered a left straight to the nose.

Qualls, at Tontam's disregard for his words, started to step between the fighters. But when Marks stopped the charge, Qualls simply shrugged and stepped back. He was confident that his rider would not have started this.

Tontam reeled backwards again. His nose was a geyser of blood. Marks saw him throw a hand up to it, confused. But the gunman simply smeared his fist with blood and bawled out a further curse. Now he stalked the younger man more warily.

Marks circled, watching for his antagonist's swing. When it came it was a right thunderbolt that glanced off his jaw, taking skin with it and jarring him. Yet it had not landed squarely and he was only beaten sideways. He recovered his balance as Tontam pressed in, certain of himself again. He stepped back from a left jab to his midsection that scarcely touched, then surged forward to find Tontam's mouth with a fast, banging right. He felt a stinging in the fist as he drew it back, and his foe spat blood through loose teeth.

Tontam's anger had flushed to a blind rage. He had not been able to make short work of this kid as he had expected, and so far he had suffered the worst of it. He knew it and was galled that others could see it. He stormed in recklessly, grabbed his opponent around the waist, and wrestled him to the ground.

As they hit the dust and grass, Marks heaved the bigger man sideways, came up on his knees, and jarred his chin with a left uppercut. Then he smashed a right high on the cheek that lifted skin. Tontam flopped sideways, then sprawled on his back. He lay there stunned and did not move for several minutes.

Marks climbed to his feet and stood sucking in air in great heaves. His mouth was as dry as cotton and his lungs burned.

Qualls came over and laid a hand on his shoulder. "What set you two off?"

"Tontam . . . wouldn't have it . . . any other way. I was out looking at his grulla. He . . . took it as an accusation. Said I was hinting he did the killing, that he murdered Smoky."

"What's this you say?" Scovil blasted. "Why would his horse suggest he did the killing? That's ridiculous!"

"Well, I didn't say he did," Marks replied coolly. "He got on the prod. I do know this. The man that did Smoky in wore boots, not moccasins. And he was on a grulla. I know that because the grulla left hair where he rubbed on a piñon. He left some scab from a sore, too, a sore on the left side of the neck. And he was with two other riders. Tontam and his grulla fit every one of these. Then, Tontam rides in here the same night, and he's touchy."

Scovil stood fuming. Then he began to reason with

Marks. His tone was condescending. "Why kid, that just can't be. Tontam an' me, we're with you all. I'm the one buyin' the herd. I was with Tontam all day. He has a hair-trigger temper, spoilin' for a fight. But, kid, Tontam never did Smoky in."

Qualls walked alongside the grulla. He lit a match and examined the neck. "I see what you see, Marks," he said as he turned back. "But still, claimin' Tontam— accusin' these folks—well, that seems wrong. What would Frank think, layin' a killin' to a man that rides with one o' the Scovils?"

Marks picked up his hat and gun belt. His fingers trembled. His knuckles were peeled and bleeding, so he went to the chuckwagon, got a little water in a bucket, and washed his face and hands. He felt refreshed. Scovil had knelt beside Tontam, talking in low tones with him. Now the gunman slowly got to his feet, wobbly at first, feeling his nose, mouth, and jaw.

"I set water in a bucket for him," Marks offered.

Tontam stalked over to wash, and Scovil stood near his niece.

"We'll be ridin' out," Scovil said to Qualls. "I'm sorry my man let his temper blaze up like that. Truth is, he has nothin' to worry about. He just likes a fight. He brought sadness on a day already filled with grief. I'll be talkin' with him. We'll go on, under the cover of night. I know an abandoned adobe a few miles along, still in good shape."

Scovil walked with Voni out by the horses and saddled his own horse while Qualls threw gear on Tontam's mount and Marks got the girl's horse ready. Working extra fast, Marks finished and walked hastily over to

154

the girl. Scovil, watching like a hawk, settled into his saddle and called out to Voni.

"Voni! Let's be goin'." He led her horse quickly to her and watched as she climbed on. Marks had no chance even for a quick word.

Tontam dragged himself slowly into his seat and led the way out. Pausing, he turned back to lay a murderous glare on Marks in the far light of the fire. "You an' me—we'll have another day," he vowed sullenly. "It'll be with guns, an' you'd better send yore last words to yore family."

Then he rode away, stiff in the saddle.

Scovil, lingering only a moment to apologize again, swung his horse in behind Tontam's and the girl's. The three vanished into the northern darkness.

13

Only a few minutes after Scovil's party lit out, Hap and Smiley rode in from their patrol. They had not met up with anything to report.

Qualls immediately sent out Wile Gaster and Shag Wootten to continue the looping sweep of the area far out from the herd.

Marks drew Smiley aside as he finished pouring hot coffee.

"Voni was here, along with her uncle and Tontam. They ate, stayed less than an hour, then left. Voni asked about you, but I didn't get to talk much with her. You savvy how her Uncle Hu and Tontam hang so close."

"Yeah, like Voni has no rights of her own. Her pa, Matt Scovil, isn't like his brother at all."

"Sorry you missed her. But I do have something else for you, from Voni." Marks produced the envelope. "Actually, Mrs. Spellman and Jackie put this in with a surprise for me. I didn't get to open it for a long time. When I did, there was this envelope too."

Smiley was excited. He opened the envelope. Marks went and tossed more cottonwood on the fire. Then he took his friend's cup to refill it. When he sauntered back, Smiley's lips had drawn tight. Marks feared it must be she'd written she didn't care for him that much after all. Smiley handed the letter to Marks.

"Here, it's all right. You read it too." The words sounded ominous, troubled. Marks turned the paper toward the fire, and, hunkering down, read it.

Dear Smiley,

I've been a stubborn fool. You were right. I was wrong. It has taken me a long time to swallow my pride. But now I have. I hope you forgive me. Now I don't know what will happen, and I am very afraid.

It is painful to admit this, but Uncle Hu is a cheap crook. He and that beast Tontam are plotting with a gang of men to steal the herd. Just how or when I have not learned. But sometime before Pueblo. I overheard them talking in Tontam's and his hotel room at Trinidad when I paused by the door. Now I suspect that Uncle Hu shot Pa. Uncle heard me sneeze outside the door, so he knows I know. He threatened to have a man kill Pa if I don't keep quiet. Knowing his gang is running free, and having seen some of them, I do not doubt what such desperate men would do. What Uncle said would happen to me if I told I am ashamed to repeat. For a while I could only think of Pa and myself. Now I see that I must think of you and those other good men. If I see you again, I hope I can make it all up to you. Should this not be possible, always know that I think of you the way I did before you went away.

Love,
Voni

Marks whistled, shaking his head. He ran fingers through tousled hair. "Well, that says it mighty clear. Good news of your woman's love, but bad news on the rest. I feel good for you, Smiley. But I'm afraid for Voni."

The wild chase, the ripped blouse, Voni excusing herself quickly from supper to retire to a bedroom, Uncle Hu and Tontam keeping vigil near her all the time, and her sobbing in her room after Uncle Hu's threatening words—all these things were clear now.

"Afraid is right," said Smiley. "I've got to tell Qualls. He needs to know. Where is he?"

"I saw him go out for a walk." Marks nodded toward the eastern prairie. "The man does a lot of thinking—and praying, I believe. The best way is alone." Bart had a lot of things on his mind, not only matters of the moment but former things—things of Bertie, Bud, a little ranch, then tragedy, and having to pick up the pieces and go on.

"Let's walk out there," suggested Smiley. "He needs to know as quick as possible."

"Sure. It's a pure shame we didn't know this news when Scovil and Tontam were right here. Had 'em right in our hands, and let 'em get away."

As they strode out a ways, rifles in hands, Marks suddenly stopped. Smiley asked what was wrong.

"Don't know. Wait a minute." Marks dropped to the ground on his chest and stomach and pressed one ear to the earth. From far off in the distance he could pick up a drumming sound. He'd paid a lot of attention to such sounds in his growing up years and knew the drone of buffalo hooves, of wild horses, of Longhorns, of antelope, of wild hogs. Smiley also fell prostrate, and they strained to make out the sound more clearly.

"Horses, coming fast," Marks finally said. "Yeah, I'm sure of it. Now they're not running any more. They're coming in slower, right toward us."

He got up and peered off into the darkness to the south. "Could be our two night patrols. Sounded like only a couple of horses."

He ran a ways farther into the night, away from the fire.

"Mr. Qualls! Mr. Qualls!"

"Yeah. Marks, that you? What is it?"

"Horses coming in. Still a ways off, coming from the south."

In a few seconds the ramrod loomed out of the blackness from the side of a knoll.

"Riders comin' in," Qualls yelled to his outfit. One rider circling the herd took up the cry and passed it on. At the camp, men grabbed rifles and fanned out to get their horses.

Then, off a ways, the clippety-clop of horses jogging on toward the fire reached their ears. In a moment a rider called out.

"Yo, the camp. Tack Laycox a-comin' in."

"Tack? What in thunder? What's Tack doin' here from the ranch? They had trouble?" Qualls lifted his voice in an answering shout. "Over here, Tack. Come on to the fire."

Tack, riding one badly lathered horse and leading another, slid from his saddle. He was gripped by a great weariness and numbed by the hours speeding northward past the Clifton House, Willow Springs, up over Raton Pass, down past Trinidad, past the Spanish Peaks, and farther north. And he'd had to zigzag in search of the herd's tracks, had to get down and look in a match's flare after darkness had come.

Qualls grabbed the cowboy to hold him erect and helped him to the upturned box near the fire.

"Jawbone, fetch coffee an' grub pronto."

"I—I near ran the legs off'n them horses," Tack mumbled. "Not far past the Purgatoire a half-dozen Utes came after me, but I got away." He sucked in a deep breath, trembling. "Whew! The herd made good time. Yo're wonderin' how come I'm here. Frank sent me."

All hands crowded near, anxious to hear.

"Thieves hit the ranch. Robbed Frank an' the missus. Got their filthy hands on the herd money—ever' dollar of it."

The news struck the men hard. There was a rumble that ran among them not unlike the low rumble of thunder. Then silence reigned for a long moment as the words sank in. Qualls finally spoke.

"They what?"

Tack took the cup of coffee Jawbone extended. He gulped down a swallow. "Yeah. Coupla nights back."

"The Spellmans?" Qualls was anxious, worried. "They all right? What about Loop?"

"All safe. That Mrs. Spellman and Jackie—Spellman can be proud of 'em. They got hold of guns and almost stopped the robbery." He swallowed more coffee, felt the welcoming warmth of the fire, and poured out the whole story.

"Hoods, huh?" said Qualls, rubbing stubble on his chin. "Any clues who they were?"

"None. Except they seemed like they was changin' their voices, like as if they was someone the Spellmans knowed. We lost their tracks on rocky ground northeast o' that new Clifton House. Never could pick 'em up again. Could be they headed for Coe's hideout country somers over toward the Dry Cimarron, or through Trinchera Pass into Colorado Territory."

"*Two* of 'em did it, though." Marks mused. He glanced at Smiley. "I wonder."

"Wonder? Wonder what?" Qualls asked, wheeling from stalking to and fro before the fire. Smiley spoke up.

"Marks an' I just opened a sealed letter Miss Voni gave Jackie Spellman. It was addressed to me, for I knew Miss Voni when I rode for Matt Scovil, her pa. Marks had the letter in a sack the Spellman ladies sent along, but bein' in the saddle day an' night an' things happenin', we never had a chance to get it read. Here, take a look. This part, folded here. The rest—it's personal."

The ramrod took the letter wonderingly. Squatting down near the fire, he read it. His mouth curled in a snarl of contempt, and he chewed his lip several times. For a long time he just hunkered there, shaking his head and blowing out air in disgust.

"What is it, Bart?" Hap finally prodded, echoed by Jawbone and several others.

"Marks," Qualls spoke at last, "I owe you an apology. I didn't want to believe this. I wouldn't let myself believe. But you were on to somethin' when you looked at Tontam's grulla. I reckon Tontam is the killer that took Smoky's life."

"Huh?" Pete Tallam sprang up. "How do yuh reckon that?"

"All the clues Marks mentioned add up now. Tontam was the killer on the grulla that waited by that tree an' rubbed its neck. Two other riders—those would be

Scovil an' Miss Voni. Scovil an' Tontam must be the two that hit the ranch. An' Tontam pickin' that fight—he was runnin' scared. Yeah, it's fittin' together now."

He tapped the letter thoughtfully. "Could be, sure as shootin' must be, that Gatril an' his pack are Scovil's outfit. Hu's men. Ike was one of 'em—picked to get rid o' me. And, no honor among thieves, mind you, one of 'em plugged Ike when it looked like he might spill the beans on the rest of 'em."

"Yeah, and it explains something else," Marks put in. "Why Miss Voni was acting so strange." He recited the incident he and Shaddo Dunlee had seen: Tontam chasing the girl across the range, and later his hearing Uncle Hu threaten her, and her sobs.

"So," said Tack, "from what I pick up, someone did Smoky in."

Qualls explained.

"What do we do now, boss?" Smiley asked. "Some of us could hit the trail after Scovil an' Tontam. Me, I'll volunteer. Voni isn't safe with them devils."

"No, none of us leave the herd," Qualls decided. "But thank the good Lord we know now. We'll salvage the herd for Frank an' his ladies. Scovil an' Tontam don't know we know, so we'll meet up with 'em soon. An' if men ever squirmed, they'll squirm."

"An' swing!" Voices came from the knot of cowboys. They were speaking the kind of justice that had been passed on horse thieves, cattle rustlers, and murderers in several different incidents around Cimarron, Trinidad, Pueblo, Colorado Springs, and Denver.

"Tontam's in for a lot more'n the lickin' Marks laid on 'im," Qualls vowed. "I agree, he needs a strong limb to exercise his neck. But we can turn 'im over to the sheriff at Pueblo. But I guarantee you, we can help the sheriff put up a guard nobody'll break through till those men swing.

"The girl? True, she's in danger every hour in this country. But she's come through so far. I'm countin' on the good Lord for her, too. We'll hope that when the rustlin' bunch hits us, we can get to her. If not then, we'll ride for a reckonin' near Pueblo.

"Our big problem at the moment is gettin' the cattle an' horses to more water. Be thankful these longhorns can go farther on less water than other cattle. But the Greenhorn an' the Muddy an' the San Carlos have water. There's a basin on the Greenhorn with a good supply. An' there's a canyon like a gun barrel pointin' into it. If the rustlers or Injuns decide to hit us there, it may take every man Jack of us shootin' our way to get to that water. But I reckon a showdown has to come sooner or later anyhow."

"Let it be sooner, then," Hap growled. "We'll be ready."

14

Marks felt the sharp sting of the morning breeze on his cheeks. He turned in his saddle to Qualls, who had led the way several miles ahead of the herd.

A report that Wile Gaster had brought in from his patrol late the night before had disturbed Qualls. And rightly so. Wile and Shag had seen the Indians before the Indians saw them, and had turned their horses back into a ravine. At least three braves passed scarcely fifty feet away, and silhouetted against cotton white clouds from where the two cowboys sprawled, they were in battle array. Stopping on a knoll, they watched the campfire a half-mile away.

The Indians had not hit the herd during the early morning hours. Qualls thought back to the twelve pony tracks he and Marks had seen, and he wondered if Coronaldo and his Utes would plot an ambush from the rugged lips of the canyon that sliced from the little valley.

"When the cattle get close to the lip of the canyon and catch a sniff of this breeze with the water smell, they'll make a beeline for the basin. There'll be no trouble drivin' into the canyon."

Qualls nodded. "But like I said, this is an ideal place

for Indians to attack. Them, or Gatril's cutthroats."

They both gazed back to the southeast. The herd, veering northeast to better water, was not yet in sight on a low-pitched ridge.

Already Qualls and Marks had traced the tracks of the three horses from the hill of murder. They had found where the hoofprints vanished on rocky terrain. But hanging a circle around the area, they had picked them up again where they were headed back to the south. They surmised that Scovil, Tontam, and Miss Voni had ridden back to the herd.

Qualls had plotted his own strategy in case his outfit rode into an attack. He'd sent Hap and Smiley from their bedrolls hours before sunrise. The two were already sprawled in the easternmost rocks along the canyon lip, and they were armed to the teeth. In the early morning darkness they had found the spot by Qualls's and Marks's painstaking directions sketched on the back of a label of a can of tomatoes. Their mounts were concealed in a clump of Junipers and scrub oak close by the nest of rocks.

Over on the other side of the canyon Wile Gaster was set up in boulders near the rim, his horse also hidden. All three of these men lying in wait could shoot with precision.

Pete, Chip, Shag, Todd, and Tack were bringing up the herd and remuda. Jawbone followed in the chuck-wagon. Riders would be able, if need be, to drop back fast and pick up more ammunition from the wagon. And Jawbone would be safer back there than in front if they ran into gunfire or arrows. He had three saddled horses tied and following behind the wagon, ready for any of the outfit or for Jawbone himself to race to someone's assistance.

Every rider, even Jawbone, moved with rifle in hand.

Marks, lifting field glasses from a brushy hill a half-mile south of the canyon's southeastern exit, mused.

"It's the way we had it figured. Even the number."

"How many?" Qualls asked. He threw up his own field glasses, careful to shade them lest sun glinting off them warn the ambushers. He began a meticulous scanning of the rough terrain to the west and up a slope to the north of the canyon.

"Twelve, so far," Marks replied. Qualls also soon picked up the procession of ponies bearing warriors across the northern ruggedness. The Indians were moving to positions along the rim. An attack was obvious. Many white men pushing into the area, especially in the nine years since 1858, had thinned the buffalo and left the redskins hungry. A herd of cattle, along with a fine remuda of horses, would be a tremendous steal if the braves could get away with them as Indians had usually made off with stock from Trinidad to Laramie.

Half of the Indians filed down a steep path off the northeastern rim and climbed via a defile to the top of the other rim. On both sides, the braves strung out along the top to shoot down on the trail drovers. All were armed with rifles, possibly taken in raids against military supply trains and settlers.

"Two thousand head—a lot of winter eatin'—an' some top-notch horses to boot," Qualls exclaimed. "That's their prize. Don't you think they'll fight for that? But with our men on the two sides, an' the Injuns not even aware of 'em, the prize can remain our own. Me, I already feel the hair standin' up on the back o' my neck."

"Give the herd a half hour," Marks guessed. "Then they should be to the entrance of the canyon."

"Then a rush to get to the water," Qualls nodded.

Both riders knew that when the front steers reached that point they would smell the basin water from the Greenhorn Creek carried on the breeze. Then those thirsty brutes would need no pointing. They would surge through the giant scoop that waters from many rains in the Greenhorn Mountains had gouged from the grassland. One passion would consume them—getting to the water.

The Indians lurked in wait, unaware of the three riflemen tucked away above them. The Indians' ponies were near them, ready for a dash to take over the herd once the red men had cut down many of the trailsmen.

Qualls and Marks felt the tightening dread that gnaws at a man before a battle. Neither wanted to wipe out the Indians who were hungry and seeking meat for hungry squaws and children. But the braves intended to massacre the trail outfit. The white men had the chance to clear out alive if they chose. Otherwise, many would die.

The lead steers approached the entrance, now a half-mile away, now a quarter-mile, then a short stone's throw. Then the bovines tossed their noses into the air. A frenzy of bawling floated up from the longhorn wave. Suddenly the leaders broke into a run. Others, by a signal clear to the longhorn kingdom, burst forward in the same instant. The thirsty critters, catching the promise of water, became a surging tide of dusty backs pouring through the canyon.

All the riders with the herd had dropped back according to the strategy. They were lost in the dust and just let the cattle go. Chip and Pete, concealed in the rolling dust, sent their mounts scrambling up a sloping bank leading to the south rim. Shag and Tack charged away toward the north side. Todd Reardon held back to protect Jawbone and the wagon.

The ramrod and Marks also were in their saddles, close to the canyon now. They cut across to join Tack and Shag and saw the two cowboys mount the crest to the rimland.

Hap saw the braves below him poised behind rocks and brush. They were ready to pick off any riders who came spilling through with the cattle. They would shed blood or themselves be killed.

"Too bad," he sighed, "but you boys are in for a jolting surprise." He yelled and showed himself as Qualls had told him to. Smiley yelled from his bulwark too. And over on the far side, Wile yelled.

Braves looked up and around, spotting the trail riders positioned above, rifles trained on the ambushers. Not a shot had been fired yet. If the Indians chose to vamoose alive, well and good. Let them keep going, away from the herd!

Suddenly a brave on the south rim whooped.

The redskins threw rifles to their shoulders. On either side of the great fissure, the Indians started the gunfire. They were dead set on stealing the beef.

Smiley had drawn a bead on one of the Indians who had taken a position along the rim. An instant after his shot the redskin buckled forward on his face. His rifle fell away. One of the other Indians saw his tribesman fall and flung a glance about him, perplexed. At first he could not spot his enemy. As he saw the puff of smoke above and swung his rifle toward the top of the lofty nest of boulders, a bullet slammed him back on his shoulders. He was dead before his body became still.

Other warriors saw the situation quickly. Having thought they could kill the trail drovers easily, they had been outfoxed. They began to scurry for different cover. Forgotten was the sniper tactic against riders they expected to knock off their horses in the canyon. But from that height where Smiley lay in the rocks, they were easy to spot.

Suddenly the three braves left along the rim had a new problem. Two trail riders came tearing in from the east, blazing away as they closed the gap on the Indians. One Indian clutched at his side where a crimson splotch had appeared. He scampered in a weaving crouch along a shallow gully fringed with brush. Then he staggered, jerked, and rolled.

The other two Utes somehow got through the flurry of singing lead from the horsemen and the riflemen above. They darted amidst brush and rocks for their ponies.

Tack, wheeling his horse about, gave chase, shooting as he rode. One of the braves reached his gray pony and started to swing astride. Just then a bullet slammed him against the animal. Loosening his clutch on the mane, the brave slid back along its body and lay twitching as the horse raced away. The other warrior, hit in the hip, saw his mount go clattering down the slope with other frightened ponies and duck into some brush. As Tack circled, the brave slipped away beyond his concealment into deeper brush farther from the battle. He would live to see other battles.

Riders on the south rimland had kept up a steady popping of rifle fire also. Then it ceased. Qualls and Marks, racing down the slope into the basin through which the creek ran, saw one brave racing south to a getaway along a ravine. Qualls threw his rifle up and let fly with a shot. The brave hunched closer to the mane as the bullet whined its song just above his black hair.

The ramrod and his companion saw that the herd had reached the creek and strung out along it, many of them hidden by the thick line of cottonwoods and willows.

Hap and Smiley came out of their hiding place, mounted their horses, and joined Tack in a gallop for the basin. Shag and Wile emerged from the south rim about the same time, both mounted. Then Chip came along with Pete, riding double. Pete's horse had buckled beneath him when an Indian's bullet hit it in the head. And Pete himself, though landing safely in brush, had taken a slug through the flesh of his thigh.

Wile, who had been comparing notes with Smiley, yelled, "We got at least nine, maybe ten of 'em!"

"All right," Qualls shouted back from near the creek. "Wile, get back an' tell Jawbone the way's clear. Watch out for any Injuns circlin' back on us." Qualls wheeled his horse. "Looks like Pete needs tendin'. Rest of you keep the cattle from overdrinkin'."

Later, as the herd grazed on the lush grass of the basin, Wile and Shag brought to camp one of the Indians flung over a saddle.

"Figgered you'd like a look," Shag said to Qualls. The ramrod and his men gazed at the war bonnet of a chief. Qualls laid the body against a large rock and took a good look at the face.

171

"Way I've heard Coronaldo described," he said, "this could be him. The chief's dress, the age, an' all."

"Must be," echoed Smiley. "They'll get another who'll do the same work, if they're hungry. Well, we don't have to worry about Coronaldo. But what about Gatril?"

Marks had ridden back to the rim he and Qualls had ascended before and during the short fight. Moving cautiously through the brush and trees, he came across a brave sitting against a rock, shot through the side. He had lost a lot of blood but was a very healthy buck, probably in his early twenties.

Having no weapon except a knife, which he grasped in his right hand, the brave gritted his teeth and waited, ready for more fight.

Marks got down, gave the peace sign to him, and took his gourd canteen off the saddle. He stepped forward, holding the canteen toward the wounded man. The buck looked at him as if in disbelief, then in gratitude. Letting the knife loose on his thigh, he slowly reached for the drink. He poured a couple of gulps down his throat, then Marks took the canteen, poured water into his bandana, and bathed the Indian's face.

Flipping the knife many feet away, Marks laid his pistol in a saddlebag and came back. He bathed the side wound. The brave would die here without help, but Marks had seen men wounded worse who had pulled through, especially strong men like this Ute. He poured liniment on the wound and bound a mud pack made from his own shirt.

The brave's pony, tied securely, was not far off in a stand of junipers. Marks brought him and lifted the Indian to his back. He used a part of his rope to strap the brave's legs under the horse's belly, then used rawhide thongs from his bag to reach from the knees to the thick mane, where he tied the thongs to fistfuls of hair. The brave would be able to stay astride his pony.

All the while, the Ute had been watching him with eyes of appreciation. Marks produced two dried apples and some jerky. The Indian ate a little, then Marks tied the rest to his wrist, using his bandana.

"Back to village," he said, and made a sign he'd seen a military scout use in Texas, hoping the brave would understand. He apparently got the idea, for he kneed the pony and plodded off to the southeast. He'd go down the slope around the end of the canyon, then circle back to the southwest to the Ute camp somewhere in the Greenhorn Mountains or the Culebras.

Marks watched him go, and hoped he'd make it. Maybe this kindness would spring back into his mind some day. White folk might live because of it. Marks was truly sorry that Indians had had to die here today. But he knew they had forced it. Had they come peaceably and asked Qualls for a steer or two, or sought a trade, the foreman would have obliged.

"Do unto others as you would have them do unto you," Marks spoke to the wind. Then the Ute was gone. Somehow, Marks believed he would live.

15

Scovil's words scalded Tontam as they jogged northward.

"I pay you to use that gun protectin' us," he said, "not to pick a fight. You made yourself look worse than ever. Guilty, like you've got something to hide. I can't figger out why you'd pull a stunt like that. Not when we stand to rake in a pile o' money off that herd."

"Huh! That Dunlee kid's been askin' fer it," Tontam shot back. He spoke through torn, puffed lips and loosened teeth. Both jaws were swollen and his tongue was cut and sore. Horse liniment and salve helped some, but he hurt from the neck up. "He horned in before when our lady here was gettin' away. Now I catch 'im nosin' around my horse, tryin' to link us with the killin'. That would've finished us off."

"No! You could've played a cool hand. In their minds, I'm buyin' the herd. It would take a lot more'n that to give 'em any sure evidence. Now they may think we're tryin' to cover up. Good thing Qualls has so much confidence in the Scovils."

"By the way, talkin' about coverin' up, you sure did a job o' bunglin' yesterday. They figgered some mistake in every move you made. Can't you handle anything right except that gun?"

He knew he could speak plainly before Voni, for his niece knew the whole plot now. She knew too much for her own good, and he'd see that she never got a chance to use that information. Kin she was, but in his judgment no kin was worth a big heap of money.

His words about not covering up well made Tontam all the sorer. "Humpf! I've always found if I handle this gun good, everythin' else is OK. I know ten men that didn't handle a gun good enough. They ain't around to talk about it. I am."

Scovil shook his head. Tontam was persuaded that his gun could take care of anything. It could take care of many things, for sure, but things often did not work out that way—not in the long run. The Espinoza killers of about four years back, who had killed around twenty white men at many places in Colorado Territory, had found that out. Tom Tobin the scout had tracked them down and brought their heads to Fort Garland as proof he'd done what he'd been asked to do. And the Jim Reynolds gang of more than twenty men claiming to be Rebel guerillas had been cut down about 1864, four of the last ones being shot by soldiers taking them to Fort Lyons. Only Jim's brother John Reynolds and another man had made it into New Mexico Territory, evading cavalry on their trail.

No, guns wouldn't do it all, not in the face of the odds. For this territory was settling, and with Fort Reynolds, Fort Lyon, and Fort Garland and an influx of farmers, ranchers, and miners who wouldn't tolerate outlaws, it took more. It took clever thinking in a deal like this. It took a cool, calculated playing of your cards just right.

Of one thing Hu Scovil was sure, fanatically sure. He would live. He would pull it off. He would live as a king on the money he made from the ruin of others.

He'd meet the men in the hidden valley within the foothills of the Wet Mountains north of the Greenhorns. They'd go over the plans so carefully nobody could foul up. Then, with everything set, they'd take the herd.

Early the next morning they followed a narrow, sometimes steep trail into the valley. The trail, passable for horses but not for a wagon, followed a deep gorge between granite ridges along the upper North San Carlos Creek. It twisted in a semicircle to the right, then dropped down a steep grade into the mountain hideout. In the valley, hills from four directions hulked over a huge basin. Several creeks slashed down from the hills, and grass grew knee-high to waist-high in many places. Once a man got a small distance into the hole, he could gaze off to the western hills and see a high mountain meadow laid into the slope. All around, the hills were green with pines, and in many places dashed with a spray of white from aspens or blue from spruce.

"It's quite a setup," Tontam mumbled. He had seen the place before, but was still awed. A few miles east, no one would dream this was here.

"True," replied Scovil. "The men with the herd could look at a dozen valleys for their cattle an' maybe never find their way in here. Not unless they got lucky. Rebel recruits, maybe five hundred or so at different times, hid here only a few years ago, and Union cavalry didn't find them till some Fort Garland men got wind o' the place. Then the Rebels scattered, and weren't able to carry out their plans to take Fort Garland and Fort Lyon, and help capture New Mexico.

"The valley's much like it must've been in the days of Juan Mace. One man, placed strategically to guard the narrow trail winding in, could stop a whole regiment tryin' to file through. Like Mace, we can hold the cattle for a time, then move 'em out by night the way we came in, or use another way I learned by North Creek toward Cañon City. I have a buyer who'll take 'em, whatever the brand."

He'd been noting the trail. An occasional pile of recent horse dung was evident. "The boys found it all right. Gatril followed directions, an' the map."

Voni slumped in her saddle. Her body was racked with weariness from the punishing hours of the day before and then the all-night trek. She was possessed of a strong body, and she had often been on a horse for many hours, but this trip was unusually long. Life with her uncle was brutal.

She shivered at his having such a lush and beautiful valley to misuse. It hurt her to think he would employ it against the hard work and sacrifice of Frank Spellman and his trail riders. Good men like Bart Qualls, Marks Dunlee, and the others might pay with their blood to gratify this greedy clutch for a pay-off and power.

And Smiley Landon—his name was the sweetest of all. Yet thoughts of Smiley unsettled her. She'd made the mistake of sending him away, or of speaking so that he did ride away. Then she had had a great change of heart. Now she longed for another opportunity. But that was remote—extremely remote. The message she had written for Smiley must have been lost. Or Smiley and the ramrod had not taken it seriously. But how could that be? If they had believed it, they could have stopped her uncle and Tontam while they were at the herd camp. She wished she had spoken up, blurted out the truth. That man Uncle Hu had spoken about would get to her pa and kill him for sure. She did not dare, yet she found herself wishing she had taken the awful chance.

Now, even if Qualls and his men were the wiser, they might fall beneath this man's vicious drive to power, for he could take his men against them unexpectedly. He held the advantages, and he'd obviously thought through the details with painstaking care.

She thought again of the ranch north of the Arkansas a ways, east of Fountain Creek. Her pa waited there, counting on the herd arriving. He and his brother Hu had gone their separate ways for a quarter of a century. Hu, he said, had been to the California gold rush and later the Pike's Peak rush. Word was he'd gathered a lot of money at times. He had shown up and acted like a man Matt Scovil could really depend on. He'd even made some generous loans to her pa, and helped him past hard times for a few months. He'd helped at the ranch and gotten it back on its feet.

Then came her pa's agreement by letter to buy cattle from an old friend, Frank Spellman. The bushwhacking of her pa followed, and he fought his way back from the valley of the shadow. He'd been so glad when Uncle Hu agreed to go to Cimarron on his behalf. He had encouraged her to go along and to visit the Spellman ladies. But as soon as Uncle Hu got her to Pueblo, a small town of about four hundred people on the Arkansas, Tontam showed up. Uncle Hu said he needed Tontam because of stories about outlaws and hostile Indians in that strip southward to Raton Pass and into New Mexico Territory. They'd hired a buggy from Pueblo to Trinidad, traveling with a party of businessmen taking a trip down there. But along the way, Tontam had started making advances.

"No more of that," Uncle Hu had said at first. And to her he'd said, out of Tontam's hearing, "Oh, I know the man is unsavory. But we can put up with that. He won't do anything much. He's a top gunman, an' he'll make sure we're safe. We don't dare lose him."

Then they reached Trinidad and the Colorado House, partly a hotel and restaurant and partly the new stage stop run by Davis and Barraclough. There she had overheard the brief conversation between her uncle and Tontam. Things began to become clear. The two were hatching some scheme to pull the wool over Spellman's eyes and get the herd and also get the money back. When she confronted her uncle, he knocked her across a bed. It was a cruel, hard blow that had left her head ringing. If she breathed a word about his scheme, he vowed, her pa would die. He had men in the right places, and he would crush anyone who might try to stop him. Besides—and she choked back a sob even now in remembering—he could turn her over to a man who trafficked in women.

She found herself trembling again, overcome physically and feeling like a wrung-out dishcloth emotionally.

She kept searching for a way to escape. She wanted to make up for her failure to blurt out the story at the Spellmans and later at the herd camp. But Uncle Hu and Tontam had slapped such a rigid watch on her that she had had no chance. Whatever she did, wherever she went, eyes were watching.

The party rode down from the pass into a "hole" that quickly spread into a vast valley. As far as Voni could tell, the basin spread for several miles east and west and also north and south. She knew that in the Rocky Mountains, distances were often hard to gauge. What appeared to be a mile might turn out to be ten. She herself had often found it to be true.

Shortly after they came down a slope into the "hole," there was an adobe cabin near the valley's east end beside a creek that wound near the base of a high ridge. Beyond the creek was a cave in the ridge under an overhang. She saw, past the sun's glistening on a million dew drops in the grass, that ten men lounged in or near the cave and also over by the cabin.

Her heart sank again. All of these were against her. She did not have a snowflake's chance in a boiling kettle. She bit her lip and tried to be brave.

Uncle Hu led the three past the men at the cave to the adobe. Voni felt many eyes like those of vultures upon her.

They went inside, where she saw a small wood stove with a high stack of chopped wood nearby. There was a crude table with a wooden bucket and a miner's pan for a wash basin. Over against a wall was a narrow bunk made out of fresh piñon poles with a buffalo hide slung over it and some blankets at one end.

"This is where you stay," her uncle told her. "An' I mean *stay*. It so happens we're not alone in this valley. There are some settlers—John Jacob Pease an' some o' his kin in a small cabin, a Mexican house, an' they're buildin' a bigger house. An' there's a Professor Boggs with his family, besides at least two other men. Since Juan Mace an' the Rebels durin' the war, these may be the first ones in here. They're good folk. I paid 'em for grazin' rights, an' I'll spread the word we've got smallpox in this cabin. My men will keep 'em away. But anyhow, you don't show yourself 'ceptin' when we give you the word the way is clear. As far as they know, I've got a herd of cattle comin' in, an' I'm a law-abidin' man who'll just be here a few days. You'll do the cookin'. So put on beans. You see a lot o' cookin' stuff in boxes over there. I brought in a big supply on burros three weeks ago."

Voni longed to collapse on the bunk. Exhaustion racked her body. But she knew better than to disobey. She found a large bag of pinto beans, poked wood into the stove, coaxed kindling into a fire, and put a large kettle on with water for coffee.

Gatril stuck his blond head inside the door. He told Uncle Hu that Mangis had brought in a deer. Voni put beans on to soak. As quickly as she could she got a meal up for the whole bunch—biscuits, venison steak, pinto beans, tomatoes from "air-tight" cans, and coffee.

It was her job to fill the tin plates with food, which the men carried outside the cabin or out by the cave to eat. Then she carried a large pot of coffee around to fill their tin cups. Making a second round with coffee, she went out across a cottonwood log bridge over the creek to the cave where three men sat cross-legged. They were dirty, unshaven men. Turning away from one to pour for two others, she heard one's remark.

"Yuh heard what he said. Tomorrow night, after an early supper. They'll be camped about a three hours' ride from here at a good lope."

She filled the two cups. Glancing past the men, she saw a bowie knife. It lay on a flat rock beside a stick partly whittled. She looked at the man closest to her to see if he wore a sheath for that knife, but from that position she could not see one on him or the others.

Later that evening the men clamored for coffee again, so at Uncle Hu's word that she could show herself outside, she brought the pot. The men at the cave hunkered at about the same place, smoking. She approached from the other side this time and saw that the knife was not on the rock. As she poured slowly into one man's cup, he was making some remark about how pretty she was. He turned to the others and they laughed. Her eyes fell on his belt and the knife in a leather scabbard. It had a thong, but the thong hung loose.

Now she knew of a way to escape—or at least a possibility.

That night Uncle Hu put her wrists in the iron clamps fixed to the corner pole at the head of the bunk. Only by lying on her side and thrusting her arms forward and up was she able to get some sleep. Before she fell asleep, she lay desperately fighting against fatigue. She needed the time to think of a way.

During the day, some number of twelve men were all about. And now she was shackled to a strong bunk formed by thick wood poles driven together with long spikes. The wood of the head posts was four inches thick. It would require an axe or a saw to cut through such a post so that she could slip the cuff chain off.

What about the bowie knife? With such a knife one could whittle away, little by little, until he cut through the thick wood.

Tomorrow night—that's what she had heard the man say. That must be the time set to steal the herd. And Uncle Hu would leave her cuffed to the bunk even as now. She had to get that knife.

16

The men had hung the remainder of the deer high in a tree for the night. The next morning, Voni fried cuts of it to go with biscuits. She put the pot on with beans again for the afternoon meal and heated water for morning coffee.

The two outlaws were squatting in the same place. Voni was careful to observe that the knife again was in its sheath. And the thong was still loose. A habit, perhaps? She took the first man's cup and held the pot to pour. Suddenly she gasped and grabbed at the pot, then ran her wrist across her eyes in a gesture of relief.

"Oh! It almost slipped out of my hand!"

"Kinda heavy, miss?" one of the rustlers asked.

"Yes, heavy, but—but I can handle it. I just wasn't gripping it tight enough when I tilted it."

The act had been convincing. It might prepare the way. Now, she thought, if that knife is there tonight, not tied down . . .

The day wore on. Voni could tell that the men were getting ready for a special ride. They were cleaning and oiling their guns, going over their saddle gear and the shoes on their horses. Uncle Hu had gotten three lanterns from somewhere, and he made sure they burned well.

As Voni prepared the early supper of venison chunks mixed with beans, along with biscuits, she got out some molasses. It took only a little of this "lick" to get her hand sticky.

The men filed into and out of the cabin. Voni loaded their plates. Then she made the rounds with coffee. As she approached the two men near the cave this time, her heart fairly pounded. Would the knife be loose? She glanced down and saw that it was.

She fought back a nervousness. Before long she'd be making the second and last round with coffee, as usual. Her act had to count. Clenching and unclenching her fingers in the cabin, she tried to relax.

She lifted the coffeepot and walked out of the cabin. After she had served the other men, she walked up the incline and noticed the two men. They were intent on their talk. She took the cup of the man with the knife last, standing at his right side near the knife. Tilting the pot, she began to pour. Her eyes closed in prayer just for an instant.

The cup was half-filled. "Oops!" she gasped. The pot slipped from her fingers and dumped into the nearest man's lap, spilling steaming contents on both men. Voni fell against the outlaw closest to her, so that he could not rise, her left hand closing around the knife handle.

"Ow-e-e-e-e!" the knife-wearer yelped. He shoved Voni away and knocked the scalding pot off his lap.

In an instant Voni had slipped the knife into a pocket in her riding pants. Now she had to hope the rustler would not check that knife sheath.

"Oh! I'm sorry," she cried, all flustered. "It—it just came right out of my hands."

The men's faces came back to normal after they had been twisted in pain at the first burning sensation. Pride in masculine toughness took command. They still smarted, but they restrained themselves.

"Ah, it don't hurt much no more," one said. "Not near as much as some o' the grub we et 'fore you come along."

"I—I guess I'll have to stand off a ways when I pour," she fumbled. "I'll go get you some more coffee."

She flew to the cabin, where she was alone. Rushing to the bunk, she fell to her knees and stuck the knife in a hole in the sod that she had jabbed out with a spoon that afternoon. Then she pushed dirt over the knife and patted the dirt down.

Taking hot water, she poured it into the coffee grounds and stirred it. She was back to the men at the cave quickly.

Uncle Hu yelled at the men to saddle up. Voni felt relief sweep over her. They would ride out before dark, and Uncle Hu was eager to move in on the herd.

"You can wash the dishes when we get back," he said to Voni. "Right now, come like a good girl. Let me clamp you." He fastened the clamps to the girl with the chain between them looped around the leg pole at the head of the bunk. "Jest so you'll be here when we get back."

"What happens to me if you don't come back?"

"Huh!" He sneered, and looked at her slyly. "What happens to you if I do?"

The outlaws hit the trail out of the valley. The

sounds of hooves had faded when Voni slid off the bunk. She got down on the dirt and dug the knife out with the toe of a boot. Kicking it toward the head of the bunk, she at last grasped it in her right hand.

The chain to the clamps was hooked around the thick post just below a top cross pole that ran to the back side of the bunk. A foot below the top pole, a second cross pole had been spiked in. To get the chain free from the post, she would have to whittle the post through within that foot.

She got on her knees and wrapped a handkerchief around the end of the blade so that her left hand could hold the tip without being cut. Then, with both hands gripping the knife, she began to whittle downward, putting some of her weight on the blade.

It was hard work. The wood shaved off slowly, but she kept at it as beads of sweat dripped from her face. The blade was sharp, thanks to the rustler. Now and then, Voni worked the blade from the bottom of her foot of space upward. Her aim was to cut through about midway between the cross poles. She also moved around the post, thinning one side and then another.

One thing about the work cheered her. She would not need to cut the post all the way through. Once she got it narrow enough, she could sit back on the ground, pull the chain tight on the upper part of the post, then kick with both boots at the bottom of the cutting area.

"Oh, thank you, God!" The task was going faster than she had expected. That aroused her to go at the work even more intensely. She threw every bit of her strength into cutting the post. It became thinner and thinner. Then it was less than an inch thick at the middle between the cross poles. She laid the knife on the dirt. Sitting back, she kicked brutally. The post snapped!

She got up quickly and slipped the chain up over the break. She was free from the bunk. She wrapped the knife in her handkerchief and laid it in her pocket. Going to the table she took brown wrapping paper from among the supplies and got leftover biscuits to stuff into her saddlebag. She also grabbed a handful of matches, wrapped a piece of venison, and got the one lantern Uncle Hu had left behind, plus her bedroll.

Her claybank grazed not far away. She swung both clamped hands together to get the saddle on, led the horse to the door, and filled her canteen from the bucket on the table. Then she rode toward the eastern pass out of the "hole," wondering if Uncle Hu had posted one of his hirelings at the outermost lip of the valley. If he had, she'd have to get past him on the narrow trail. She was ready to lay the quirt to her horse for a wild dash past him.

Peering into the darkness, her heart pounding, she reached the crest of the trail and rode down clear of the pass. The walls of granite were dropping behind. Uncle Hu apparently had assumed he needed no guard by night, at least not until he had the cattle there.

She recalled the way they had slanted to the left and then curled upward around to the right to drop down into the valley. She also knew that these, the foothills of the Wet Mountain range, were to the west of the area the herd must pass on its trek north toward Pueblo. The men would be camping now. She should point the claybank about due east as far as the rise and fall of the foothill country permitted. And she might bend a bit to the southeast after a while. The trail drovers should be perhaps fifteen to twenty miles from the hidden valley.

She remembered mention of a Peter Dotson and his wife who had a ranch headquarters on San Carlos Creek a few miles from where she rode. But she did not know how to find the place except by slowly following the arroyo of the creek and working through trees and brush that formed a line along the watercourse. She felt a pull to take the slower route and seek out this man, whom her pa had said had been a U.S. marshal in Salt Lake City back in the 1850s. He was a good man, and he would help.

But concern to try to reach the herd, possibly more quickly, drove her to more open country to the east. She rode at a lope, trying to make out the terrain ahead and letting the claybank's night eyes bear her across the miles.

To her dismay, heavy clouds began to mass. By the looks of things it might be a ruthless downpour. Flashes of forked lightning lit up the area, and awesome claps of thunder rolled among the swells of a gently rolling prairie. Juniper, scrub oak, piñons, and brush beat at times against her legs and arms.

About two hours further in the blackness the rain began to lash at rider and mount in great sheets. Voni had drawn on her slicker. She felt the sensation of blindness in the dark of night and the greater blackness of the driving deluge. She slowed the horse, for his footing was more precarious where many gullys dashed their water load through the land.

She knew there was no way to warn the trail crew now, no way to get into the camp. But surely, in a storm such as this, all hands were around the cattle. Smiley would be out there. And how could those longhorns, easily spooked as they were, be held back from a stampede in this fearful lightning and thunder?

Slumping over her horse's neck, she felt very tired from the physical harshness and the emotional ordeal. She felt she was about to fall into a dead sleep, and she wished that Smiley was there to hold her.

17

Jawbone was ready to issue his welcome call to supper. The men would have to eat fast and get out around the herd with others already there. Then the drovers heard a rumble of thunder. In seconds a gully washer lashed the land.

"Mount up an' get out there," Qualls shouted. "Be ready for anything!"

Slickers had already been pulled on. The few men at camp hit their saddles quickly and flashed out to join their companions. Jawbone scurried to get his supplies from under the wagon. He tossed firewood back into the sling cuna to keep dry.

Scarcely had the party left the campfire when a volley of gunfire joined the roar of the storm. At first it was difficult to discern from where the gunfire came. The rain's relentless, deafening drone was all about. Then the longhorns, already frightened at the thunder and lightning, broke westward. Cattle at the eastern side, panicked at the gunfire that was nearest them, sprang forward in terror. In a second the herd plunged at breakneck speed into a night black as pitch.

Marks was swept toward the southern side of the

leaping, shoving, scrambling tide. His horse, by some instinct known to the animal kingdom, had caught the direction of the seething mass even before its rider. A drum of hooves and crash of brush rose even above the roar of the rain. As his mount tore through the black depths he judged that the longhorns were veering to the northwest, skirting a ridge that lifted to the north. Beyond was fairly open terrain, though gutted by small, sandy washes that would now be running with water. His horse had reached the left side of the stampede and was very close to the cattle. Due to the rough rise and fall of the prairie, the mount could smash down at any second and Marks could be rolled on. But he'd pulled through stampedes before, and his job was clear. He had to try to swing the cattle back into a mill. Forgetting his own peril, he drove spurs to his rangy roan, thankful that a surefooted night horse sped beneath him.

Thunder was still blasting in the sky. Rain poured as if the Arkansas River had been scooped up and spilled down. Unable to see anything, not even his hand that gripped the reins, he sensed he had reached the front left flank of the pounding herd. His yells and those of others did not turn them. In a flash of lightning he glimpsed two other riders trying valiantly to veer the animals into a mill.

Behind, he thought he heard a popping of guns again. He had no idea where the rustlers were or where others of his friends rode except those two the lightning had shown him.

The longhorns hurtled on over low brush. They splashed into and over watercourses the storm had filled. And as they themselves poured over the land, Marks was stung by the burning heat of their bodies. He saw the foxfire of lightning running riot on the critters' horns.

Another bolt of lightning flashed. This time it lit up the terrain ahead. Marks gasped. In the shelter of a cottonwood on a little knoll beyond a raging wash a claybank horse hunched with drooping head. And on the ground beside the mount was a woman. In the ragged flicker of lightning, he read the terror in her face. Hitherto unaware of the rampaging herd because of the storm's din, she now looked at the threat of death. The herd would reach the top of the knoll in a few swift jumps.

Longhorns were amazing among cattle. Raised in a wild land that called forth the keenest instincts, they possessed an uncanny ability to dodge objects even in total darkness. But the closely massed bovine bodies and this terrifying darkness gave no guarantee of their swerving around the girl. The herd's leaders were pressed on by the mighty torrent behind, and all were crazed by their panic at the thunder, lightning, rain, and gunfire.

Marks rammed spurs into his horse. The roan jumped clear of the mad plunge of cattle and lunged up the incline in breakneck stride. Another flash of lightning danced on the knoll. It afforded Marks another look at the woman. She was desperately trying to slip her foot into a stirrup as her horse wheeled and screamed in panic. Leaning off to his right and fixing a powerful grip on his saddlehorn, Marks encircled the woman's trim waist in an arm of steel. He swept her up and away as his horse sensed the urgency and blasted on, dropping down the far side of the knoll.

Snatched away, Voni realized what had happened. A

trail drover had hauled her up right in front of the hot breath of the long-striding cattle. She felt her boots and riding trousers slap against brush, and grabbed quickly for the cowboy's waist, clinging for dear life. Desperately holding her lest she fall, Marks reined the roan out to the left, felt the impact of a gully and the sudden stagger of his mount. Then the trusty horse saved himself from a horrible spill, sprayed water, and gained the far bank of mud. He surged on at a slant away from the cannonballs of cattle.

Several jumps later, wide of the herd, the horse landed in another invisible gully where water rioted. He staggered and then rammed into the far bank. Both Marks and the woman were flung off, tumbling in brush and mud.

Unhurt except for bruises, Marks came up in a crouch, searching for the woman. The darkness was so thick he felt as if he could cut it with the bowie on his belt.

"Where are you?"

"Here—over here."

He threshed about through the pelting rain. Finally his fingers felt her hair. She was lying beside a thick patch of brush that must have cushioned her fall. He grabbed her and carried her to safety. They clung to each other, half-protected from the rain by a small tree.

They could still hear the herd pounding through. That, so close by, was louder than the rain and the hum of the runoff. Somewhere farther back along the herd, two more gunshots sounded.

"Miss Voni, are you all right?"

"Yes, I'm all right. I don't think I would have recognized you if it hadn't been for the lightning, Marks." Voni sank against Marks, seeming to fall limp in exhaustion.

"The stampede—I reckon your uncle and his gang are the ones doing the shooting."

"They rode out to steal the cattle. I—I got away. I hoped to get to you in time—to warn you."

"Much obliged. But the way this storm broke, the cattle were primed to run anyhow. Before that thunder a while back, they were like cocked pistols with hair triggers, ready to be fired."

Another flash of lightning illumined the area. In this lingering flicker, Marks saw the wrist clamps, and that explained the tinkle of the chain he'd heard.

"Vonie, you stay put—right here. You ought to be safe. I've got to help the others, but I'll be back."

The herd had by now all streamed by, at least the main part of it. Stragglers and off-shoot groups of longhorns might be scattered.

All that shooting had only scared the cattle more. Qualls, like many a good cowman, had cautioned his outfit against firing before or during a stampede. "It'll only frighten 'em more. You let 'em hear yore voices, the familiar sounds, an' try to get 'em circlin'."

Marks scouted around for his roan. After plodding through mud and grass that sank beneath his boots, he found the horse beneath a piñon, his head down, breathing hard from his strong effort. Speaking calming words, Marks eased up and gathered in the reins. Walking the mount to test him, he decided that he was not injured from the gully spill. The shoulders and legs were not torn, and the legs walked well.

"Good job," he spoke to the animal as he swung up.

"You tore over some rough country and kept your feet. Didn't fall till we were clear. I owe my life and Voni's to you."

He worked his way at a jog out to where the southern fringe of the herd had raced through. He was thankful that the rain had lessened to a strong drizzle. After some searching on the back trail of the stampeders, he heard an urgent yell not far off.

"Bart, answer me! Bart! Bart!" It sounded like Hap's voice. Marks reined back to the southeast as far as he could sense it in the dark.

"Hap? This is Marks."

"Yo." Hap was by his side in a minute. "Can't find Bart," the other man said. "He was right with me, but a bit behind. He yelled, 'Let's go back an' deal with 'em.' I pulled out to go with 'im. Then, in that blast of rain, thunder, an' shootin', I thought I heard Bart yell again. I had no idea where he was. He sounded like he'd been hit. I took a graze on my arm myself."

"Let's keep up the search," Marks said grimly. "And let's hope . . ."

A short distance later they called again for the ramrod. A six-shooter barked a little off to their left. Riding that way, they were sure they heard a gasping voice.

They were almost on top of him when they vaguely made out Bart's form sprawled on the lip of a wide wash where shallow water still gurgled. When they dismounted and knelt, they saw one of Bart's legs hanging over the bank.

"Hit bad," the segundo said through gritted teeth. "Got me from behind—in the back."

Marks fished for a match inside a rawhide pouch. In its flare, protected from the drizzle by his hat, he and

Hap pulled back Bart's slicker and saw the broadening blotch of crimson on his shirt.

"We'll get you back to the chuck wagon," Marks assured. "We'll get the herd back, too."

Qualls set his teeth against the pain. "My time may be almost up. If—if it is, all's well with me. Havin' peace way down deep with God is—it's a wonderful thing. But I don't want to go right now. Too much I'd like to live for."

"Yeah," Hap agreed. "You hang on, Bart. You're one of a pattern, an' we want you around."

"There may be another Bertie—another Bud," Marks said soothingly. "You could have a lot of years."

Silently, Marks prayed. And knowing Hap's sentiments from their chats by the fire, he figured the man was praying too.

As fast as they could, they rigged up a travois to carry Bart on. Hap struck out for camp with his horse pulling the travois. Marks went back to fetch Voni.

The rain had ceased, and Jawbone would no doubt have another fire blazing. But he'd be out in the darkness somewhere, or sticking close to the chuck wagon for cover if the wrong men should ride in. And he'd be in a shooting mood.

A man of foresight and experience, Jawbone already had a place cleared in the chuck wagon when they got back. The nasty weather, treacherous ride, and the shooting had moved him to think he'd better be ready with a place where a wounded man could rest. They laid Bart there, and Hap fished the bullet out with a pair of slender tongs Jawbone kept in the wagon. Bart was biting down on the thick bull hide of a whip, and he passed out about the time the tongs fixed on the lead.

"Ahhhh," Hap said grimly, his leathery features grizzled with the strain of his task and concern for his friend. "He lost a lot of blood, but he'll pull through. The slug caught him at an angle. Hit his hipbone mighty hard an' put his leg out o' whack. Must've caught 'im when his horse was climbin' out of a deeper gully."

"Will he rest OK?" Jawbone asked.

"Hope so. But I've got more to do. He's a stronger man than many, an' that'll help. But let's don't kid ourselves. The main thing he's got goin' for 'im is the work o' the good Lord . . . his will, an' the care he shows to one o' his own trustin' family."

Jawbone knew something of the background of this cowboy treating the wound. He walked away shaking his head in gratitude. "Makes a man thankful," he muttered, "Bart havin' Hap to tend 'im. I don't know why the man left the doctorin' profession he'd started out in an' came to nursin' cows. But it's a good thing he's here."

Voni sank down on a dry blanket Marks spread under a thick canopy of tree limbs.

A few minutes after Hap had extracted the bullet, Shag Wooten limped into camp. He was leading his horse, which had its right shoulder laid open with an ugly gash. "Hit a sharp rock," he explained. "Threw me onto a steer, but I leaped off an' dove clear. Twisted my ankle when I fell into a gully."

Before Shag did anything else, he got rawhide strips, a long doctoring needle, and liniment. Then, using the light of the fire, he sewed up the gash on his horse.

Marks took Hap and Shag and combed the long area where the herd had run. They carried lanterns. They found Pete Tallam's broken body lying in a heap near a mesquite tree. His face was torn by mesquite needles—

some still bristled in his flesh—and his shirt front was soaked with blood from a bullet wound in his side. They lashed his body to Hap's mount, and Hap rode double with Marks.

Not long after that, Shag yelled them over to him. He had come on to Chip Morrow's body. The rider's horse had rolled hard on him after hitting a rocky bank and veering away. Securing him to Hap's horse also, they sent Shag afoot back to camp leading the animal.

A dozen or so steers came under the searching lantern light. Some were trampled in gullies where they'd gone down, others had to be shot because of broken legs, shoulders, or hips.

The search also led to one of the rustlers, who lay dead by a scrub oak. A bullet hole in his neck gave grim witness that one of the trail riders, returning the fire, had found the mark. Marks and Hap laid the body across Marks's horse, and the two drovers doubled up on the mount Shag had left, heading back to find the camp.

Tack Laycox had made it back to camp by the time they rode in. His horse had stepped in a prairie dog hole, and he'd led the badly limping mount back. Seeing no hope for the animal, he sadly unsaddled and put him out of his misery. That heartbreak came on top of the ones he'd already learned about.

The men huddled near the fire and poured down hot coffee. They were worn and disconsolate. The toll had been high with Qualls badly wounded, Pete and Chip dead, and Shag limping. Wile Gaster, Smiley Landon, and Todd Reardon were missing, and the herd and remuda gone.

When Marks had come back and dismounted by the fire, Voni walked over and glanced quickly from him to Hap. Dread haunted her eyes, and she was afraid to look at the bodies brought in.

"Smiley hasn't come in," Marks told her, realizing what was on her mind.

"Ohhhh!" She put both hands on her cheeks and closed her eyes. "I am so afraid he may come in like these."

"Hope for the best," Marks replied. "We'll scout the rest of the night. Smiley, Wile, and Todd know what they need to do. They may be a long way off, afoot. Or they could be trying to hold smaller bunches. Then again, they may be trying to find out where the rustlers are taking the cattle."

"They're in real danger, then," she shuddered. "I know that gang. They are worse than rattlesnakes."

"Yeah." He led her closer to the fire. "But Smiley and Wile and Todd know how to handle themselves. Besides, we need to trust our good Lord. Then we'll do the best we can too."

Hap called Marks to the chuck wagon.

"Bart's conscious again," he said. "He's askin' for you."

Marks bent over the weakened ramrod, whose face was lined with suffering as well as concern.

"I'm gonna have to do a lot o' sleepin'," Qualls said matter-of-factly. "Hap told me what's happened. We're not finished, but the men need a leader—a man that's healthy."

"Yeah, we've got some good men," Marks replied. "Any one of them—"

"No, Marks. It's *you*. I want you ramroddin' while I'm down. I like the way you handle yourself. You're a man now, an' I want you to take these men and get the herd back. Deal with Scovil the only way he'll understand."

"Boss, I—"

"No objections," Qualls cut him off. "That's how it'll be!"

Marks grasped the man's hand and swallowed hard. "Like you say, Mr. Qualls. I'll do my best."

"I know that. Now get to it."

Marks turned, shifted his hat on his head, and bumped into Hap. The man wore a huge grin, and thrust out his hand. "You got my total backin', Marks. Hop to it."

"Thanks, Hap. There's others could do this."

"No! You heard Qualls. He may be down, but he knows what he's doin'. The men—every man Jack of us—will be behind you as we are Qualls."

Marks straightened up, his shoulders broad. He turned to face the others, and a surge of confidence began to fill his mind. There's a time when a man is born. This was his time.

Marks looked up into a sky where wind had carried the clouds away. Stars twinkled up there. A few strides away from the wagon, he was talking with the One who had made those stars, who knew how to head up everything.

Hap told the others about Qualls's choice. Not a man balked, despite Marks's youth. He was a man in their eyes, and they were as one, men living by a code, and part of that code was being true to the brand.

"Hap, Shag, I want you to ride out with me and comb this area again. We'll be back by daybreak if not before. If no success, we'll grab a bite to eat on the run, then hit it again with the help of the sun."

Voni came over as he reached his horse.

"I know where they're taking the cattle," she said. "I was a prisoner there. After they rode out, I used this to get away." She lifted a bowie knife. "I—I think I can find the place in the daylight, or after a search. But the trail into the valley is narrow, through a pass where one man with a rifle could mow down a dozen."

She described the hills at the pass and into the Wet Mountains. "It was called Fisher's Hole, and now Mace's Hole."

"So," said Marks, "we'll have to figure a way to get in there while we're covering the country for any cattle . . . or Smiley and Wile." He winced at the clamps and the chain, which they'd been so busy they had not removed. "Tack," he called, "you and Jawbone get these off while we're scouting. But keep alert. Some of that gang might try to finish off more of us. They might try for the chuck wagon."

He rode out with Hap and Shag. And as he rode, he also clung to another trail—to the place where he always found the best help.

18

Smiley heaved a sigh of relief when the herd slowed to a trot, then a walk. The shooting had ceased some time back, yet the rain continued for a while in a drizzle. And darkness about him remained so black a man might think he could bucket it and sell it for boot polish. But he stuck with the longhorns as close as a cockleburr clinging to a steer's tail. He could hear the tromp of many hooves on mud or slushy grama, the slap of legs against brush, the click of those great horns, and occasional yips of riders. Of one thing he was sure: The voices were not from men of the brand for which he had risked his neck.

Except for those noises, he and his horse might be alone on a tiny patch of prairie, ready to step off into limitless space.

Curiosity dug spurs in his thoughts. Had any other trail hands stayed with the herd? He assumed they must have. Hunched in slickers with hat brims yanked down to protect their faces from the pelting rain, men would look much alike in the less frequent lightning flashes. Normally, a cowboy knew some companions so well he'd recognize their ashes in a whirlwind. But here, about the only way a man could recognize another was by his voice.

Giving his mount free rein to move with the sea of backs rippling unseen in what must be the Greenhorn Valley, he kept his mouth shut except for a disguised yip now and then. A man aware of the general nature of country where he trailed cattle, he'd paid attention to remarks at the Qualls campfire. He knew he now rode somewhere to the northeast of the famous Zan Hicklin ranch, the Greenhorn on Greenhorn Creek.

As the story went, Hicklin and his wife Estefana, a daughter of New Mexico's territorial governor Charles Bent, had ranched on a Mexican land grant since the late 1850s. Bent had been killed in a Taos uprising of Pueblo Indians and Mexicans in 1847. Hicklin had become one of the biggest cattle and sheep ranchers between Pueblo and Santa Fe. And word was he'd helped cavalry of both the Union and Rebel armies during the late war, supplying beef and serving as a guide. Smiley knew that Qualls and the outfit could count on help from Hicklin in finding the cattle if the rustlers got away with them. Hicklin himself had dealt quick justice to men who stole from him.

But Smiley knew he must follow with the herd for now. If more of his crew were still here as he was, they could assert themselves sooner or later. But where was Qualls? Was he hurt? Or had he dropped back to pull the men he could together for a strike later on? And where were the night raiders taking the cattle? From the direction he reckoned they must be going, they'd wind up somewhere over by another ranch he'd heard about, on San Carlos Creek—that of a Peter Dotson, whom he had met. Dotson, like Hicklin, would be a rancher to count on. The man was well-respected, having been a U.S. marshal in Utah for several years before coming to Pueblo.

Yes, these were cattlemen to count on. But then Smiley wondered what the rustlers had up their sleeves. They must have some plan they figured would work, some way to get the herd hidden before daybreak, when passersby might spot them. Smiley had heard of a valley, a place where Confederate recruits from the Colorado Territory hid out with their leader, a John Heffner. The place was Mace's Hole. It was, as the stories folk told around campfires had it, a place entered by a narrow pass. Some had reckoned as how it was no wonder Mace had evaded wrathful stock owners for years seeing as how a defender could hold off many trying to file in. Smiley wondered if Mace's Hole was a place where rustlers might hide out again.

Up ahead Smiley saw a very pale light, a small glow, but too big to be a cigarette. It seemed to be waving, like some sort of signal lantern.

Smiley rode for many hours through the night. Shortly before daybreak he saw the blur of a lantern again, swinging right and left like a signal. He heard a voice through the early morning dimness.

"All set. Let 'em file in thisaway."

Smiley had been aware of his horse ascending a gentle slope for some time, for his body had slid back in the saddle and the horse was plodding harder. The lantern receded and the cattle began to hesitate as if bunching and pouring into a narrow gate. Smiley had to stop and wait as the longhorns found their way in before he came up to the entrance. Now he felt his stirrup scrape against a rock. Reaching out to his left, his hand touched a wall. Then he brushed against the limbs of a tree and was almost raked from the saddle.

Smiley knew that he was entrapped with longhorns ahead and longhorns behind. The lantern up ahead seemed to have climbed as if the rider was on higher ground or on a rock watching the animals file by. Smiley was approaching him. He did not want to be recognized, so he worked his horse to the right, getting a longhorn to his left between him and the man hoisting the lantern. As he rode past, he bent down, letting his hat brim hide his face. Suddenly he was past, and the guide had not cursed or cried out. Either he was undetected, or the man had marked him and would watch for him once they got into the hideout.

The trail looped around to the right after the steep grade, and Smiley knew he was making a descent down a rather treacherous slope.

In the faint morning light he became aware of a creek off to his right. Then his horse veered a bit to the left off the trail, and he knew the animal was swishing through long grass. He also heard the brush of many cattle legs moving through it. A rider yelled far ahead.

"We made it! We're in!"

Smiley saw another lantern light come on not far ahead. He had to plot his move quickly. These were not only rustlers—they were cold-blooded killers.

The herd was spreading out fast. Ahead, Smiley made out a man hanging the lantern on some kind of shack. Between himself and the lantern, he caught sight of two riders pressing toward the shack.

He glanced back and saw nobody in the darkness. Only more longhorns were coming. Then he swung to his left, came to a precipitous hill, and skirted it a ways, getting within a stand of trees that would cover his move. Reining farther up into pines and a steep climb, he let the horse work its way around the far shoulder of the hill. He judged that he was making a loop to the far side and cutting somewhat back toward the way he had come into the basin. The ridge appeared to be jabbed like a giant thumb into the outlaw stronghold.

The vague light of dawn was beginning to etch out shapes of rocks and trees. He got down off the horse, a weary animal after the hard run and the many miles. As to himself, he gritted his teeth at the protest of his body when he tried to stretch aching limbs to full length. It was painful to shake out the stiffness, and he kept blinking his eyes that had been afforded no rest for twenty-four hours. Resolutely, he began a slow and difficult trek, picking his way along the ridge.

Reaching the top, he found himself and his mount well-hidden in pines, spruce, and many kinds of brush. Grass was here, heavy with moisture. Below, he could make out the blurred shapes of cattle. The creek flowed past the outlaw camp and out by the entrance to the east. According to what he had heard, it could well be the San Carlos.

Satisfied that he was alone, he stripped the gear from his mount. The horse was glad to shake itself free of whatever wetness it could. Smiley wished there was a dry place in dust or grass for the horse to have a good roll. He sought out tufts of dry grass beneath rock shelves and near some pines. The animal was pleased to get a vigorous rubdown.

Staking out the horse in a thickly wooded spot where he could still manage to find some grass, Smiley went to take up a vigil. He wondered if the other drovers were in the same situation he was in. By now, morning light had made the camp scene clearer. Down beyond the ridge he was on, lantern light was plain at the doorway of an adobe near the creek.

As he watched, three other men rode along near the creek from his right to his left. They approached the adobe. Suddenly he was aware that one man was of massive build. It was Wile Gaster.

Peering down, Smiley determined that Gaster did not have his pistol in his holster. And no rifle butt jutted upward out of his saddle boot. The other two men rode slightly behind him, one on either side, their rifles over saddlebows ready in case Wile tried to make a getaway.

The captors must have spotted Gaster's six-foot-five frame during or at the end of the drive. A man who had formerly ridden with outlaws but who had turned completely back to the right with the help of Marks's brother Lonan, he had proven himself in every way Smiley knew.

The outlaws had Gaster dismount near the adobe and prodded him inside. Smiley did not see him after that, so he surmised that they had made him a prisoner.

"So," the cowboy on the ridge mused, "it's up to old Smiley. I've got to find a way outta here, get help, or this is it for Wile and Voni. Voni—where is she?"

He noticed a cave at the base of a granite bluff across the creek from the adobe. Two men tromped across a crude bridge of cottonwood logs and mud. They hunkered down inside the cave mouth to spin up cigarettes. Smoke was issuing from the cabin chimney, and no doubt the rustlers were ravenous for breakfast after a hard night's work.

Then two men stepped out of the adobe—Scovil

and Tontam! The two were gesturing as if in anger. Scovil slammed a fist against the adobe wall and wheeled, pacing. He pushed his hat back, scratched his head, and gave the indications of a man perturbed.

Smiley wondered if he was angry at Voni. Was she too slow getting breakfast? Not likely. It was very early yet, and the rustlers had been here only a few minutes. He let his eyes rove over the grassland below and saw no sign of her claybank.

He glanced to his right. Down the ridge to the east, just up from the foot of the grade that would lead one to the narrow pass out of the hole, he caught a flicker of light. It was brighter than the light of morning. Was it the gleam of the sun on metal, a gun barrel? Then he saw. A man sat atop a boulder, almost hidden by pine branches on either side. He was smoking, and beside him on the boulder he had just laid a rifle. Smiley could see that the rifleman would have plenty of time to cut riders down, since they would have about three hundred yards to cover until they broke even with him.

When rustlers went into the adobe and came out with loaded plates, Smiley felt the grab of hunger. He could almost taste the coffee, made the way many drovers liked it—thick enough to float a horseshoe or make a spoon stand up. He gathered up some piñon nuts and patiently worked to extract the nuts for a small meal.

A man came to relieve the guard so that he could go to breakfast. Another outlaw rode out to the entrance, disappearing around a twist in the climbing trail. Soon a different man rode back on a different horse. A second lookout was maintaining a vigil over the valley spread out to the east, northeast and southeast of the hideout.

"Ahhhh," Smiley mumbled. "With two good shots

cuttin' down on any that venture in, it would take a mighty large bunch to get anyone in alive. The rest o' the rustlers could take care of 'em then."

He knew that in order to get out, he'd have to find a way past two sentries, spaced several hundred yards apart. And his best chance would be at night. He was game—make it out or die trying. He found himself mumbling some words he had heard many times: "This poor man cried, and the Lord heard him, and delivered him out of all his troubles."

19

Smiley, keeping up his vigil through the day, saw a pattern in the periods of guard duty. Both the outlaw at the entrance and the rustler below on the ridge were relieved every four hours. The guard times were no doubt this brief so that the men would stay alert. New men came out around ten in the morning, two in the afternoon, and six at night. When they came, they carried canteens of hot coffee. Smiley had crawled close enough to the guard on the hill to hear the new sentry at six o'clock mention it.

One thing provoked satisfaction: Nobody bothered to check on the guards in between these changes. Maybe they were aware that if they slept on duty they would pay with their lives.

Down in the outlaw camp, some of the men had resaddled before noon and driven the longhorns farther into the valley. One of them yelled to another, relaying orders. "We're takin''em to Second Mace. Swing around the settlers' places."

A few hours later, some of the riders were back from Second Mace, wherever that was. Smiley wondered if it was a second valley or pasturing area farther back, more hidden. If flanked by steep mountain sides, one or two men could keep the longhorns there.

After the six o'clock change in guards, Smiley stole back up and saddled his horse. When the old guard down the hill had gone back to the adobe to wolf down his supper and to rest, Smiley worked his way on foot down the slope to the guard's boulder. In his previous stalk down, he had made careful mental notes of objects that would afford him cover when he made his big move. He had also observed places not to step, spots where he might betray his presence on crackling twigs, pine cones, or shale that would give way. Now he called upon his utmost patience. He took plenty of time to close the distance. A man who knows the slightest mistake can mean death can afford to go slowly.

The glow of the guard's cigarette in the deep tree shadows was a marker. Then the sentry broke out in a binge of whistling. Smiley was thankful, for this helped cover any suspicious sound.

"Don't make a sound!" The authority of his voice and the sudden jab of a gun barrel in the back proved totally effective.

"What the—?" the guard grunted. Smiley took the rifle from the boulder and lifted the revolver from its holster, then relieved the sentry of a belt knife. "How'd you get in here?"

"There are ways," Smiley replied. He made him lie down on the pine needles back of the boulder and bound him with utmost care.

"Ah! The North Creek trail. But I thought they put a guard there too."

"Too bad about him." Smiley played along. "All of you are done for. Hangin' around with stolen cattle is gonna get you a lastin' place to hang around. You've got a good neck for it, too."

He finished binding the guard's hands behind his back. "Your man out front's careless too, like you."

"Yuh—yuh slipped up on Donk too?"

So, Donk was the other guard's handle! Smiley had gotten some information he wanted. It might come in handy. "He should've stayed where the boss told him."

"Ah, Donk! Why didn't you stay up on that rock outcroppin'? Best view of the valley there anyhow!"

Smiley grinned slyly. Now he had more information.

He gagged the guard with a rock knotted in a bandana, secured with rawhide thongs so that he couldn't work the bandana up or down. Then he used his rope to lash him to a pine.

That done, Smiley led his horse down the slope to the trail out. Stopping at the San Carlos, he let the mount drink, and he himself got down and drank, then washed his face in the cold mountain water. Filling his canteen, he rode up the trail between the towering ridges that wore whiskers of trees and brush. He held the horse to a walk that would cause no thought that he brought danger. He neared the part of the hill that would most closely overlook the valley to the east.

"Hey, what's up?" A figure had stepped out astride the trail about ten paces ahead. In the moonlight, Smiley could see a rifle cradled in the second guard's arms. He kept the horse to a walk. Grunting, he let air out of his throat as if disgusted, letting the horse close the distance.

"Ah," he drawled, making the best imitation of the voice of the guard back behind as he could manage. At the same time he put a rasp into his throat so that he would sound like he had developed a problem in his voice. "Jest a night ride, Donk. Boss sent me . . ." He put a low grunt into the words, as if irritated with the duty.

"Night ride?" Donk Bodeen lowered his rifle, stepping to the side to let the horse draw even. As yet, he could not discern the color of the horse. "Whar to?"

Smiley jerked his pistol from concealment behind his leg. "Make a peep an' I'll drill you!"

"Huh?" Donk froze. There could be no mistaking the threat, and he did not recognize this voice. At close range, the rider could not miss. He decided it was not a good time to peep. "Yeah . . . don't . . ."

"Slide your hand to the top o' the barrel, an' hand it up slow, butt first."

"Shore . . . yuh got it."

"Now, turn around." Smiley leaned out, lifted the pistol clear of leather, and stuck it in an open saddlebag. Then he holstered his own pistol, slid his rifle out of its boot, and pushed Donk's rifle into the boot in its place. A few minutes later he had the guard bound with a rope off his own horse, which was tied to a tree back in a curve of the ridge wall. He also looped the rope around Donk's neck and held the end of the rope as they rode away.

"We're gonna ride hard," Smiley said grimly. "Try any trick an' you'll get the dumpin' o' your life."

The moon provided some light now. They loped across the prairie. But they had been on their way only a couple of minutes when Smiley hauled his horse to a stop and shouted for Bodeen to do likewise. Riders had cut in on their path ahead.

"Who goes there?" Smiley called out.

"You're covered and surrounded," a voice yelled back.

"Marks?"

"Smiley? That you?"

"It's me, in good health. But hungry enough to finish off a whole steer."

The riders quickly came around the two. Five trail drovers and eight other men sat their horses, and Smiley could tell in the moonlight that six of the strangers wore Mexican sombreros.

"This here's Pete Dotson," Marks explained. "Has a ranch not far off, and he's here to help, with three good men who work with him. Over here, this is Zan Hicklin, from his Greenhorn Ranch, and three of his men."

"Both of us, Pete an' me, know that valley about as well as any men alive," Hicklin said. "There's also a way in from over to the north, but it's a long ride around. And there's other ways through passes farther west."

"No need," Smiley said. "We can go in right here. They had two guards, only two. I got both of 'em. One's tied up, an' here's the other."

"Wondered where you were," Marks said. "You and Wile. You seen Wile?"

"Yeah, saw 'em take him in an adobe just inside the valley."

"We can ride right in?" Dotson asked. Getting an affirmative answer, he whistled. "Isn't that good news!"

"How about the folk livin' in the hole—Mace's Hole?" Hicklin asked. "The Peases, the Boggses, an' the rest?"

"Don't know about them," Smiley replied. "All I heard, from the hill where I hid out, was one o' the rustlers yellin' they were takin' the cattle to a second place, an' not to bother the settlers' farms."

"Naw," Bodeen said sulkily, "we didn't hurt no settlers. The boss wanted to be on friendly terms with 'em."

"Better be true," Hicklin said firmly. He was tall in his saddle. "We can really make long necks of any that treat these good people bad."

Smiley told them the layout inside the hole. In fewer than five minutes they were riding to the pass, armed to the teeth. They would get there before a change of guards.

Smiley now knew that Voni was safe, staying with Mrs. Dotson until this matter was settled. He also knew he had a new ramrod, Marks. And he was glad for both pieces of news. But he grieved at word that Qualls had been badly wounded and both Chip and Pete had been killed. Hap had said that Qualls's fever had gone up during the wagon trip to the Dotsons, but during the late afternoon it had begun to drop.

Now, to rescue Wile Gaster and the cattle.

20

Scovil lay awake on the bunk. The fat wad of greenbacks he'd stolen from the Spellmans was stuffed in his coat pocket. He needed to hide the money and provide himself with protection, a special guarantee. Should Tontam make a greedy bid to take it, Scovil would be able to save his own life. Tontam would not likely kill him as long as he alone knew where the money was. The same would go for the others, none of whom Scovil could really trust. He swore under his breath. That was one of the curses of this business—no honor among thieves!

Silently in the darkness he felt the bulge. Ah, it felt good. Tontam more than once had cast a lusting eye on the coat for more than the share Scovil had given him. The money would take a man a long way, to a lot of high living such as Scovil craved. And Scovil knew Tontam, knew him better than Tontam realized. He'd carefully checked Tontam's background for a good while before he engaged him on this job. He had found out that Tontam was a living wonder with a revolver, one of the fastest and surest west of Abilene. He also knew that Tontam had been involved in robberies. What was to keep the gunman from trying for the big wad if an opportune moment arose? The man had no more scruples about murder than a cat lying in wait for a bird.

Scovil sneered in the blackness of night and the deeper darkness of the adobe. He himself would not hesitate to murder—not when he stood to gain. Why should Tontam, who had chipped out ten notches on his gun butt, this man who got a twisted thrill out of watching a man squirm?

He arose with the utmost stealth. Both Tontam and the prisoner, Wile Gaster, were snoring with the force of a Conestoga rumbling over a rocky trail. Inching the door open very slowly so that the creaks would not be heard above the drone of the San Carlos, he slipped outside. From his saddlebags near the door, he drew a small satchel out of which he had taken the greenbacks. Now he shoved the wad back into the satchel. Tontam had not stirred in his bedroll.

The rustler boss crept northwestward along the ridge. A long stone's throw from the adobe, he climbed beyond an overhanging shelf of rock. There he found the old Ute Indian path he had learned about from Braid Mallas many months ago. Mallas had assured him that nobody else in the world, of the white race, would know about this trail to the east. It was a trail centuries old, but well-hidden.

Scovil followed it. The trail struck sharply upward to a cliff far above. Despite the steepness, a horse could struggle up. Once high on the bluff trail, Scovil pursued it the way he knew in a twisting, dipping, rising course for about three hundred paces. Finally, rounding a bend, he halted and caught his breath. The trail was only wide enough for a man, or a man leading a horse. From here, he climbed up a sloping, towerlike jutting of granite about the height of a three-story building. His fingers reached for the sure grips he'd learned. Finally he pulled himself up and crawled into a cave about three feet high and five feet across. Utes had rested here. Animal bones lay about the floor, as well as the ancient leather of a moccasin and burn marks near the base of the wall from an old campfire. Mallas had mentioned a number of other places Indians had used, different from this cave in that boulders had been placed in rings, sometimes with tree trunks, for fortification and shelter.

On his hands and knees, Scovil dug loose rocks from the floor and buried the satchel and a loaded derringer. Even if Tontam came here, Scovil had an ace in the hole.

Finished with his night work, he lowered himself carefully down the rock face. Smugness tingled his big frame. He could come back to that pile of money. And should anybody foil his plans and search him, he would have no proof on his person.

He thought of the trail through the pass by the San Carlos. North of there, this Ute path wound out of the hills. But it was well concealed, and he'd even covered it over with brush as a guarantee no one would see it. Below him now, far down the dizzying height from the trail, below the granite tower and cave, were ragged rocks and murderous boulders.

Suddenly he jerked about. A rock had rattled somewhere along the trail back. Startled, Scovil tried to pierce the darkness with straining eyes. The noise had not been far away. He edged forward but saw only the vague line of the ledge trail and the hulking rock face above it. The noise could have been a wolf, a mountain cat, or some other animal of the Wet Mountain range prowling at night. On his earlier search of Mace's Hole and its environs, he'd spotted a wolf. So he shrugged it off.

Quickly he made his way back, ready with a lie in case Tontam had awakened. He came to the exit from his trail beyond the rock outcropping and walked a ways toward the adobe. Glancing about, he saw a man squatting near a bush. It was Tontam.

"Tontam! What are you doin' out here?"

"Horse woke me up," the gunman said. "He was rubbin' on the 'dobe. I saw you was gone . . . figgered you was out for a walk or a smoke. Me, I'm doin' the same. Where you been?"

"Me? Oh, just sittin' up on a rock, figurin'. Makes a man feel peaceful, hearin' the night sounds. Like you said, I couldn't sleep anyhow."

Tontam spun up a cigarette, lit it, and took a long drag. Over to the southeast, where horses were picketed on good grass not far from the adobe, one of the animals nickered. Another horse answered from farther over toward the slope approaching the entrance pass.

Suddenly Scovil was uneasy. "I thought the remuda was over that other direction."

"Yeah. Sounded too close to be one of the guards' horses." Tontam had become tense. They stood listening. In the moonlight, Scovil thought he detected a movement, then a rock clattered.

He wondered if some of the settlers were out wandering at night. But he had greater fears. Perhaps the guards had fallen asleep. "I feel somethin'," Scovil said ominously. "You don't suppose they found the valley, got past the lookouts . . ." He started striding toward the adobe. "The girl—she might've remembered enough. Or one of the trail outfit could've seen where we brought the herd in an' pulled back. I told the men to watch everything."

"I dunno," replied Tontam, moving swiftly with him. "It's a long shot. I don't think the guards would go to sleep, not at the risk of what we threatened. An' nobody could get past them."

"Still, sounds like someone's over there," Scovil agitated. "Come to think of it, I don't remember hearing the shift come back after ten o'clock."

Tontam bit his lip. He hadn't either, and he'd been awake, despite the fake snoring when he lay there wondering when Scovil would hide the money.

"Just in case," said Scovil, "I'm gonna slap a saddle on. After that, we can check the men at the cave. If somethin' went wrong, we can be set to ride—fast."

"Ride where? If they've come in past the two guards on the east, we'll have to head north to the North Creek way."

They got to their horses and hastily saddled. Scovil was still thinking. He knew it wouldn't hurt to let Tontam in on the Ute trail. The money would still be hidden. Tontam would not guess it was far above their heads as they led their horses along the ledge. And he still had need of Tontam's gun—for a while. Later, a well-placed sneak shot could take Tontam out of the picture in some lonely place. After things settled down he could ride back to the concealed trail. The money would be waiting.

"I know it now," Tontam hissed. "There are men over there. I heard the clink of a bridle." He swung astride his horse. "Maybe—maybe the girl went to the settlers in here instead of out to find the Spellman outfit.

Then the guards might not even know they're out there."

Scovil swore under his breath and wished he had taken care of his niece a surer way. "Better rouse the men at the cave," he whispered. "We may need their guns."

Tontam walked his horse around back of the adobe, making as little sound as he could. Only two men were sleeping at the cave. He shook one of them and hissed for him to be quiet.

"We've got trouble, but keep quiet! Scovil an' me, we think there are men out there ready to attack."

"Huh?" The men scrambled out of their bedrolls and pulled on their clothes. "How come jest two of us?" one asked. "Should be four! The two that finished guard duty at ten should be here!"

"Yeah," Tontam snorted. "Somethin' bad wrong for sure. We may have to make a run for it—every man for himself."

The two rustlers snatched up their rifles and slunk out to get to their horses beyond the adobe. Before they got halfway to the adobe, a voice rang out.

"You're surrounded! Stop and surrender!"

They dug furiously for the adobe, still determined to get away. A voice boomed from one of the rear corners of the adobe: "Halt, or I shoot."

Tontam settled back into his saddle, sank spurs to his mount, and raced in a loop around the adobe hugging the shoulder of the horse. Aided by the darkness, he made his getaway.

Guns cracked out in the night. One of the rustlers racing from the cave tumbled into the wet grass and lay still a few steps from the adobe. The other stumbled, regained his footing, but pitched into the grass far from his horse. It was Gatril. His gun had flamed orange toward the corner of the adobe. Now it swished harmlessly through the tall grass. His body twisted in pain as he sprawled there, unable to rise.

Scovil had lunged inside the adobe. He found Wile Gaster sitting on the hard floor. The man was bound hand and foot. Gaster knew now that his outfit must have gotten into the hole. As Scovil bolted inside, Gaster desperately rolled, throwing his enormous frame into the outlaw boss's legs. The chief tumbled headlong, and Gaster rolled again, hoping to pin the man down and hold him until help arrived.

But Scovil sprang up too quickly. Gaster felt a gun snout jab him brutally in the side and slide to his back. He stopped his roll. Moments later, after Scovil cut his leg thongs with a knife, he was on a horse, bareback.

"This is Wile Gaster I've got," shouted Scovil. "Shoot, an' you may hit him!" Then Scovil mounted and led Gaster's horse. When he reached the Ute trail, Tontam was waiting nearby. Scovil wondered about that, and about the noise he thought had been a wolf. Both outlaws led their horses up the difficult slope, Scovil going first. Gaster was between them. At last they reached the ledge path above the long death plunge.

Riders converged swiftly on the adobe. Marks and Smiley led the way in pursuit of the three ahead, found the trail, and scrambled up.

Tontam, moving behind the other two, rounded a bend in the cliff trail. Pausing, he fired back around the rock face, chipping stone near Marks's face. From behind rock at another bend, the drovers returned the fire.

"Ahhhhhh! I've been hit!" Tontam gasped just loudly enough for Scovil and Gaster to hear. He sank back into a recess in the rock where the boss could not see him.

"How bad?" Scovil asked.

Tontam's groan was pitiful. "Bad—real bad. Right in the gut." He groaned again. "I—I'm dyin'. Not a chance. Go on—git out while you can!"

Scovil smiled slightly. He had always planned to dispose of Tontam when he no longer needed him. This was taking care of Tontam for him.

"Well, nothin' else I can do but go."

"Shore. I'm finished anyhow. Go, then!"

Tontam peered around the rock, trying to make out the shape of a trail rider. A sly grin crawled up along the curves of his jaws. He tapped the rifle barrel against the rock at the bend, drew a shot from those back there, then fired his own gun.

Shots ceased. He heard the thud of hooves on stone ahead of him. They drew farther and farther away. Tontam was exultant. He had outsmarted a fox, and he believed he would have the last laugh.

Another shot sent its echoes along the rock wall. Bits of stone fell from the bend nearby, some clattering on the ledge and some falling far away down the precipice.

The trail men knew they could not advance along the path as long as Tontam could pick them off. They waited.

"Give it up," Marks yelled. "It's just a matter of time anyhow."

"Time," the gunman said. "Time, he says." He fired two more shots. "I'm waitin' right here. Take a step out on this ledge an' your burial place is a long way down."

Tontam leaned his rifle against the rock recess, confident that no one would risk coming on along the trail.

Carefully, he worked his way up the jutting granite, hidden from the men back there. Reaching the cave, Tontam poked around the sides, believing Scovil was far away.

His fingers clawed at the floor of the cave. Nothing. Only loose rock, possibly some ashes, and animal bones. He snarled. Then as he pawed rock out in a loosely packed area, his fingers touched something different. He felt, exulted, and drew it out. There was a derringer wrapped in a cloth, then a leather case. Inside it, his fingers caressed the bills of money.

Gripping the satchel, he made his way down the rock slant. "I'm still here," he called out to the trail drovers. "You see, I have a lot of patience."

"So've we. We'll have the herd—and you." Marks had recognized Tontam's voice. "You murdered Smoky. Remember? Or does that kind of thing even linger in your memory? You're the man on the grulla with the sore on its neck."

Tontam swallowed as his mind raced back. But he yelled back in contempt. "So what? You haven't got me."

Silence reigned. Some kind of night bird broke that silence, fluttering along the wall far below.

Tontam had been studying a break in the rock ledge near his feet, well out of sight from the pursuers. The split was about four or five inches across and looked to be deep. He reached far down into the fissure and found it deeper than he could touch. Drawing out a cord, he tied a small rock to it and lowered it. It struck bottom about five feet down.

He got up and eased along the ledge to his horse. He'd laid a large rock on the tips of the reins to hold the animal. Now he pushed the satchel into a saddlebag. He dug into another saddlebag and began to draw out what he wanted. He'd taken these from a miner with whom he had worked for a time in the Pike's Peak area. The miner had left to go to Missouri, but Tontam had followed secretly and killed him. His body well-hidden, he'd returned to the mining area with several hundred dollars the man had slaved for. Giving up the work, Tontam had drifted. But he'd brought these and hidden them in Mace's Hole. Today, after getting back from the rustling raid, he'd ridden out alone and gotten them from the cool place.

Sticks of dynamite—and he'd learned how to use them. Sometime, he'd figured, they might come in handy, might be the edge he needed.

He moved the horse farther away, put the rock on the reins again, and returned to the ledge in front of the rock tower where the cave was. Using his cord, he lowered the sticks one by one into the crevice, spacing ten of them one after another, out from the wall toward the cliff face.

Some clever man had come up with a new way to make explosives a year or so ago. Tontam remembered the miner's story, based on a newspaper article. A man named Alfred Nobel had perfected the dynamite sticks. He'd been working to improve explosives for years, dealing with nitroglycerin and trying to reduce the danger and the accidents.

"Well, Mr. Inventor," Tontam cackled, "thanks for these sticks. How 'bout 'em workin' this time, like last time, eh? I can blast a mighty big chunk out with ten of these!"

Working quietly, he lit the fuse line on the tenth stick and it began to sputter.

He was a safe distance away on the ledge path in time.

"Hey, I smell smoke," said Smiley. "Somethin' burnin'. What in thunder?"

The explosion shattered the serenity of the old trail. A huge mass of ledge was blasted loose and fell in many pieces into the rock bed below. Far down from the level of the trail, a hole was torn out about twelve feet along the path. At the bottom, the rock slanted downward toward the outer face of the cliff.

"Well, he has us this time," Marks said. "We'll have to go back the way we came into the valley. But by that time, they'll have a long head start. Hold on, Wile. We're coming."

"Where will they head?" asked Smiley. "They've still got several hours of darkness, an' it'll be hard to pick up their trail once they get clear o' the hills."

"Three horses," replied Marks. "That'll make it easier. Don't even think of losing them!"

21

Scovil, in spite of being ousted from the valley, rode with confidence. He was a man nourished on his own delusions. His was the confidence of a man who thought he had the world by the tail on a downhill pull.

"So I lost the herd," he said to himself. "But I've got all those thousands hid. Later on, I'll find a way to rob brother Matt, too. Or I'll get my hands on the payment for the herd in the care of those trail drovers. It'll be a long way back from Matt's ranch to New Mexico Territory."

He thought of the gang that had been coming together over the months with William Coe. Some of those men he knew. He might entice them to join him for a job that would give each of them an inviting cut.

"One way or another, I'll be back," he mused. He threw a glance over his shoulder at the Wet Mountains. "I'll get the satchel. Livin' in a good disguise, I can slip away, go back to the Trinidad area, an' pull a new bunch together. When I come out of this an' make it back to the east, or to California, I'll be fixed up real good."

He grinned back at the big captive whose horse he led. "Know what I've got in mind for you, cowboy?"

"Nothin' would surprise me—not with you," Wile replied. The man hadn't even fed him while he was a prisoner. He'd simply said, in contempt, that a man that big had enough to go on without food.

"Oh, but this will be different." Scovil laughed. "This won't be with a gun. Much quieter than that. The crick'll be deep after the rain. But the water runs peaceful there. Spot I have in mind nobody ever comes to. When I tie the rock to you, much bigger than you, an' get it rollin', it'll drag you down the bank to the deep place. Think of it this way. When you hit the water, it won't take long. How's that sound, big man?"

Scovil chuckled. Then he fell back again into his own thoughts. What a fortunate man he was with Tontam out of the way. Tontam had trained his gun hand and relied on bullets. Scovil had exercised his mind and depended on brains. Tontam was wrecked on an old Indian trail. Scovil lived to seek new trails.

Suddenly the two riders pulled up. They heard a boom somewhere in the Wet Mountains. The exact direction from which it came was not clear. Scovil gazed back, wondering. He'd heard that kind of boom before, in various places in the hills near Denver. Was some miner working back in there, beyond the rustler hideout? He had no inkling that Tontam even knew about dynamite or carried sticks. This information had never come up in their talk.

Wile Gaster was a desperate man. He had entirely different thoughts. The warning rang in his mind: Now or never. He knew the creek with the huge boulder might not be far away. Getting set for a sudden lunge forward, he drove powerful toes into his horse's belly. Instantly beside Scovil, he lifted one boot and whacked the outlaw hard in the rib cage. The impact of the huge leg and the momentum of the lunging horse slammed the cattle thief out of his saddle. He landed in a jolting fall at the side of the cow path.

Wile threw himself off his horse as Scovil's mount sprang forward to stay with the other mount. The big man landed close to Scovil and scrambled quickly to his feet. Seeing the cowboy hauling himself to his feet, Scovil tried to sit up and clawed for his six-shooter. It had just come clear of leather when Wile's right boot kicked the wrist. The gun went flying off into brush.

Scovil bawled at the pain, then surged up with fury, starting toward Wile.

"Come ahead. I'll kick yore legs out from under you," the cowboy warned. He backed toward the horses which had stopped about fifty paces further along the path, reins dragging.

"I'll get my gun an' we'll see," yelled Scovil. He wished he had the derringer he'd planted with the satchel in the cave. He charged into the brush, frantically feeling for the pistol.

Wile spoke soothingly to his horse and reached its head. He stooped to grasp the reins in his teeth, and stepped over to mount. Letting the reins slide through his mouth until he had enough to reach up to a mounted position, he leaped. Getting a massive right shoulder and right leg well over the horse, he was soon fully on.

Raking spurs to the animal, he started forward. Scovil came up with his pistol just in time to try a shot as Wile's horse bolted. The bullet whined dangerously close, but the horse rounded a brushy bend and was out of Scovil's sight.

Wile straightened up, glanced back, and realized

after a bunch of jumps that Scovil was not pursuing.

Scovil sputtered, furious that the darkness had delayed his finding the gun.

As Wile topped a knoll, he stopped and surveyed the dark land. His friends were back in the Wet Mountains, or coming from there. After circling back far to Scovil's flank and riding on a ways, he heard a horse coming. He saw a lone rider coming at a lope. The horseman passed not ten feet away, and Wile thought he looked like Tontam. Wile wondered how the man had managed with his stomach wound.

He breathed a sigh of relief and set his horse to a jog. He hoped that the next men he saw would be his friends.

22

The trail led to Pueblo. It was early morning, an hour after sunup, when Marks, Hap, and Smiley rode down the muddy Santa Fe Street toward the Arkansas toll bridge. They passed John Thatcher's store at the corner of Fourth Street, then the El Progressive Saloon at the corner of Third. At the corner of Second Street, they saw the sign of the two-story board building, the Valley House. Smiley said he knew George Stout, the proprietor, and added that the mail coach from Dodge City pulled up here.

They left their horses out front under a cottonwood and went in, hungry for breakfast and seeking information.

Stout greeted them and stood talking while a Mexican woman went to bring food.

"Hu Scovil an' Lacy Tontam, huh? Well, I do remember they were here about two, maybe three weeks back. I haven't seen or heard of 'em comin' back, but I think I can find out for you. Give me a few minutes." He went out and soon was back with a freckled-faced boy of about twelve.

"Rusty here works at the stable an' sees just about

everything that goes on along the street. Says he saw Tontam."

The trail drovers turned from a hungry attack on ham and eggs.

"Shore," the boy said. "I saw 'im when he was here before, an' he was here this mornin'. I'm up by five, an' I came through an alley. He was knockin' on Lilly's door, back room of the saloon. She came an' asked 'im in. While I was away from the stable she came an' got her dapple gray. They rode out goin' west, I'd reckon toward her place. She has a shack about three miles out, not far from the river."

"Probably havin' breakfast with her there," Stout said. "Lilly's got a lot of friends, men that go out there."

They got up to leave, left money, and headed for the door.

A man of about sixty had been sitting at a table with a lady who might be his wife and a younger woman.

"Excuse me, gentlemen," he said, getting up quickly. "Could I have a word with you?"

Marks looked back and saw the elderly lady smile. The younger woman, dark-haired and kindly of face, had turned about. She was looking at the man who had gotten up.

The man led the way out by their horses, beneath the cottonwood.

"I'm Moss Jensen," the white-haired man said. "My wife and I run a wagon freight line between Julesburg, Denver, and here. A friend, Dottie Draper, has just come from Independence by way of Abilene. We overheard you tell Mr. Stout you were with a Frank Spellman at Cimarron. Well, you see, Mrs. Draper is also an old friend of Barton Qualls and his wife, bless her soul. We hear Mrs.

Qualls is deceased, and Mrs. Draper's husband died late in the war, serving as a lieutenant. She was trying to start a dress shop in Abilene when Mr. Qualls met up with her again just a few weeks ago. Well, you see, they are both lonely people, and Qualls told her he wanted to see her again. I think they saw they were very interested in each other. Now, her plans for the shop in Abilene changed, and she wants to start a shop in Pueblo."

Marks glanced at Smiley and Hap. "This all sounds good, doesn't it, men? 'Course, it's up to Mr. Qualls and Mrs. Draper. Was that the lady sitting with you and your wife?"

"Yes, that's Dottie."

"Hmmmm. If she's anything like her looks, Mr. Qualls may have himself a jewel."

"Oh, she is. One of the finest ladies my wife an' I have ever known. Real homespun, and a true Christian lady."

"Just one hitch at the moment," Marks said. "You see, Mr. Qualls was—well, he was hurt when rustlers attacked us to get our herd."

"Hurt? How bad? Where is he now?"

"Shot and lost a lot of blood. But Hap, here, knows his doctoring. Mr. Qualls is getting better. Resting at the Peter Dotson home on the San Carlos, where the stage-coach stops."

"Well, we'll go right out there," Jensen said. "Mrs. Draper has been a nurse. Wouldn't she love to take care of him!"

Lilly's shack had been built of pine boards on the leveled top of a small hill. Pines, piñons, scrub oak, juniper, and tall brush afforded seclusion.

The three riders tied their horses well back and crept near the dwelling. Then Hap circled and worked in from the rear. Smiley and Marks approached from angles to the two front corners. That way, each could watch the door in front, yet not be in a direct line of fire if Tontam should burst from the doorway.

Two horses stood switching flies under a pine a few feet from the corner of the cabin.

Tontam had not known the pursuers were hot on his trail, so he was under the delusion that he could take his time. Smoke issued from the chimney, and Lilly was getting up some breakfast. At the moment the three could hear a lot of raucous giggling.

"Tontam!" Marks yelled. His voice was freighted with authority. "We've come for you!"

The saloon woman suddenly fell very quiet. A chair scraped on a board floor. The next sound may have been the banging of a whiskey bottle on a table. After that there was just a low sputtering of curses.

"Who wants me?" a voice yelled.

"You murdered Smoky. You know who wants you."

"That you, kid? Dunlee?" The door opened just a crack, and Tontam was obviously looking the situation over. A woman's face appeared in a window, checking as well. "You need a lot o' backin' to do yore work, kid? Three agin one. Is that yore style, huh?"

"Most men of your kind run up against more than they can handle sooner or later," Smiley put in. "Give yourself up, an' you'll get a fair trial, more fair than you dealt Smoky."

"Smoky? Who was Smoky?" Tontam yelled back contemptuously. "Why does Smoky bother you so much?"

"Maybe you wouldn't savvy," Marks rejoined.

"Smoky was a good man. Rode the right trail, worked hard. Everybody liked him. Not a scratch on his name."

"Who cares? He wasn't very good with a gun, not when it came right down to it."

"You never gave him a chance. You took his guns and shot him down like a dirty coward." It was Hap's voice.

"Cut the talk! You sayin' I'm yeller? Now's the time to back that up. How 'bout it, kid? Jest you an' me, alone? How 'bout that? You can prove yo're a man, kid. Or is it you who's yeller?"

"No need to prove that," Marks shouted back. "Lots of better ways to prove that, like doing a man's work, living a clean life like a man oughta."

"Hey, you lecturin' me, kid? If you can't prove it my way, you can't prove it at all. I'm comin' out, an' Lilly here can tell the town how you couldn't do yore work alone."

Marks glanced at Smiley. "Looks like this is the way it has to be."

"No! No!" Smiley exclaimed. "You can't go up against that mad dog, Marks. He's a professional gunman. You don't have to do this."

"I'd give anything to avoid it," Marks said slowly. "But not my honor. It was never the Dunlee way."

"Yeah, but . . ."

"Hey, kid, yore friends afraid fer you?" The taunting voice lifted, and then Tontam cackled. "So am I. Didn't I tell you the other night? Next time it'd be with a gun. You ain't gonna let your friends talk you outta it. Not you. Not a Dunlee. I'm comin' out now. Jest you an' me first, Dunlee. After that, yore friends can have a try as soon as they like."

"Get on out, then!" Marks shouted. "I'm waiting. Are you going to show?"

"Hah!" The contempt carried out around the hill.

The door banged open, but only halfway, shielding Tontam fully from Smiley on Marks's right and from Hap who was farther to the right. Tontam shook his right hand, limbering it. His cheeks and lips still bore scabs from the fistfight at the cow camp. But the lips still could curl back in a sneer of disdain.

Things can whirl in a man's head at such times. Images can pass so swiftly. Marks remembered a story Ma had read to the children long ago, and which he himself had read since. The characters were David and Goliath. The bigger they are, the harder they can fall. In the depths of his being he was trusting in the same God David had.

"So, me an' you, eh, Dunlee? There's been near a dozen, but never one this special. A Dunlee for breakfast. A *Dunlee!*"

Marks knew the man thought himself so fast and accurate that he could knock down one man, then use the half-open door as a shield while cutting down the other two.

"Three graves on Lilly's hill!" Tontam cackled.

"Still waiting," Marks said coolly. Smiley was amazed at the iron nerve. This kid was as cool as a mountain creek in the early spring. No wonder Qualls had named him to take over the trail crew.

The gunman noticed too. The men he'd faced had usually shown their fear in some way—a quiver of the voice, a trembling of lip, a twitch of the cheek, a look in the eyes. Men like Gatril and Mangis would find a way to back down, to slink away. But this kid showed plenty of sand. Cocky as Tontam was outwardly, this worried him. The Dunlees were fast.

"Draw!" shouted Marks. Then Tontam made his move. Dunlee's right hand whipped up in a blurred speed. His wrist flicked. The gunman, a sneer still on his lips, snapped his .44 out of its holster. It came up smoothly in the same speed and polish that lay behind the notches.

Then Tontam's body reeled backwards in the doorway. Something small and burning had stabbed his chest like the red-hot piercing of a rod from the fire. The impact shocked him, threw him off, kicked him back. He caught himself on the doorpost, tried to hang on, labored to bring his gun back up.

His gun spurted flame at the dirt outside the door. His legs gave way. Swaying for a full second trying to prevent the buckling, he pitched backwards flat and hard on the boards of Lilly's place. The gun clattered harmlessly across the boards.

Smiley had his gun half-drawn when he saw the gunfighter hurled back. The fight was over—over in one blinding moment.

Hap stepped forward and stared wonderingly at Marks. He saw the gun poised in the young ramrod's hand, still emitting a thin curl of smoke. Glancing at Smiley, he caught his friend's shake of the head.

Marks strode slowly forward, letting his gun drop to his side. As he reached the doorway, he saw Lilly fall to her knees beside the sprawled Tontam. A deep sadness gripped his heart. Smiley put an arm around him.

"I reckon," said Smiley, "that Smoky would've said justice was done here. An' that's the way the law would have to see it."

Marks nodded. He understood that.

Tontam, gamely hanging on, looked through glazed eyes at the men who crowded around. In his stare it was clear that he just couldn't believe it. It was as if he were in a dream.

"Scovil and you robbed the Spellmans," Marks said as he hunkered down by the man's chest.

"Yeah," was the labored admission. "Money . . . my . . . saddle. Scovil . . . thinks . . . he left it hid . . . the rocks above . . . dynamite."

"Who shot Matt Scovil?"

"Hu . . . Scovil. Wanted . . . the ranch."

Tontam was dead. Marks looked in the gunman's saddlebag slung over a chair and found the satchel of money.

"Special friend o' yours?" Hap asked Lilly.

"Special? No. Men come, they go. Some of 'em have more money than others." She shrugged and turned away.

"One thing we'd be obliged for," said Marks.

"Sure. I'll swear it was a fair fight."

Stopping at the door, Marks turned back. "One other thing. Don't mention what he said, I mean about havin' the money. We haven't rounded up this Hu Scovil yet. He's the man that led Tontam in this sorry business."

She nodded.

They tied the body on the gunman's grulla and rode back into Pueblo.

242

23

When Marks and the other drovers trailed the cattle out of Mace's Hole, Hap stayed behind. He camped outside the secluded valley where he could keep field glasses on the two ways in, the regular trail and the Ute trail. The Spellman riders had located the exit of that second trail when they spotted some dry brush Tontam had shoved aside.

This was a cat and mouse game for Hap. Hu Scovil still figured that the money was buried in the mass of rock. The prize seemed to lure him out of hiding once he was sure the trail riders had all pulled out. He had no way of knowing that the Spellman men had found out about the cave.

After Marks and the others went on north with the longhorns, Hap stuck to his lonely vigil day and night. By night he moved up close to the Ute path. He was a patient man, whether as a doctor, a cowboy, or a watcher. And he savvied it was worth it to Spellman and to Matt Scovil for him to wait this out.

On the fifth night after the herd filed out of the valley and came together with cattle that had broken off in the stampede, a rider approached. He came slowly, quietly, in the vague light of late dusk which would soon deepen into darkness.

Hap, overcome by weariness due to a lack of sleep, had fallen into a doze. But he snapped awake when a hoof kicked up a stone not twenty yards away. He saw the rider as he got down and moved brush aside. Then the man vanished, leading his horse along the ascending trail.

The bulk, outlined against a rock slab, was the shape of Voni's Uncle Hu. Somehow, to a tired man, his coming at last was a welcome sight.

"He'll have to come back past me," Hap mused. "He doesn't know the trail is blasted away right under his money cave. But, he'll find out, an' back he'll come." He was ready to step from hiding behind the rock and take Scovil a prisoner.

Scovil led his horse for a ways. Then he tied him to a stout bush at a point where the trail was wide enough for the animal to turn around. He'd come back to the horse in just a few minutes.

He made his way alone. He knew the trail well, though it was very dark under a sky laden with black clouds. All he had to do was keep close to the sloping rock on his left, which the path hugged. Much of the time he paid scant attention to the trail itself; he figured he could almost follow it blindfolded.

He chuckled every step of the way. His plans were working out after all. True, he had lost the big herd. But nobody had laid a hand on him. He had a big pile of money waiting up there—money he'd gotten an easy way. Now things were even better, for he would not have to share any of it and take it back by murder. All of his men were dead or in custody. The fat roll of green-backs was making his mouth water in expectation.

The darkness was oppressive, but this pleased him. His feet easily found the familiar trail without the help of his eyes. He quickened his pace, his excitement almost a frenzy. He was looking up, eyes straining at the massive black bulk of the rock tower. Dark as it was, his hands found the gripping places he had carefully memorized.

He was only two steps away from his payoff, just around the bend. He surged forward and planted his full weight on the spot, his body thrown into the stride. His foot stepped on air, and shot down.

"Ahhhhhhhhhhhhhhhhhhhhhhhh!"

A horrible scream shattered the night, followed, far below, by a thud. Then all was peaceful again.

Hap waited. His eager ears picked up the screech of an owl and the soft pad of a wolf that loped along a ravine. Far away in the mountain haunts an unnerving scream sounded. He wondered if it could be one of the mountain cats, but it sounded like a human cry.

Not long after the scream, Hap heard the sharp ring of horseshoes striking stone. He figured Scovil was coming back, leading his horse. Hap crouched beside a tall rock, ready to reach out and haul the man to the ground. He sprang out.

He stood gazing back into the blackness of the trail. Only the horse had returned. The animal, whose reins Hap grabbed, trembled and tossed his head as if spooked.

He wondered if the scream had been Scovil's. But he kept his watch, curious. The night passed, but the outlaw boss did not come back from the Ute trail. Hap, weary but fairly well convinced now, welcomed the light and warmth of a new day. And with that light he walked up to satisfy his curiosity.

Marks and his men delivered the herd to Matt Scovil a few days after they filed out of the rustler basin. Scovil, still held to his bed, threw his arms around Voni and put his full blessing on her wedding plans.

"I lost a son to the cholera," he said. "Always hankered for another, an' I'd never get a better son than Smiley. You two can have the choice bench land north o' me. Some of the finest grazin' this side o' Wyomin'."

Scovil gave his word he'd raise the full amount of the money for the herd. Buyers were on their way who would pay top dollar for beef to sell to the miners who crowded into the mountain towns.

Smiley strode out of the bedroom, his face shining. Marks grabbed his hand and pumped it. "Two weddings coming up," Smiley said. "You heard what Mr. Qualls said when the Jensens and Mrs. Draper moved him to Pueblo. I reckon he's gettin' over the pain of losin' his first wife. I think this Dottie's gonna be just what he wants."

Marks sauntered outside and stood gazing southward toward the far-off Arkansas River. Farther away, he knew, was the Spellman ranch. In a couple of months, Josh and Jackie would stand before a circuit-riding preacher, too.

Marks thought again of the girl in the picture, Mandie. Some day he wanted to meet this Mandie. He glanced to the east, for she was there, in Virginia. For now he was jubilant for the friends who were planning lives together.

Out of the corner of his eye he glimpsed Smiley and

Voni. They strolled, hand in hand, to a hill behind the house. Marks knew their words were pleasant, even if he could not hear them.

Voni's cheek found a place she cherished against Smiley's chest. The two stared out across the Colorado vastness to the bench range that seemed to beckon.

"The cabin's there, you remember?" she said dreamily.

"The cabin, yes. I can see it nestled in the cottonwood grove, wildflowers all around. And lots of room for us to build."

OTHER WESTERNS
from Living Books

Westerns in the Living Books series feature the action and excitement you expect from Westerns—plus a concern for moral choices and personal integrity. In the great tradition of American Western novels, Living Books offers you quality stories that show—with realism and compassion—the age-old conflict between good and evil.

THE DRIFTER by Gilbert Morris. War-weary drifter Jim Reno finds himself caught in the conflict between the greedy Carrs of Skull Ranch and a group of small ranchers. Though tired of violence, Reno is determined to free the rancher from Skull's exploitation. Number 1 in the Reno Westerns Series.

TREACHERY AT CIMARRON by Jim Ross. Ruthless killers and a beautiful scheming woman haunt the Cimarron range, seeking a rancher's gold. Marks Dunlee learns of the plot and plans a daring rescue. Number 1 in the Dunlee Westerns Series.

AMBUSH AT VERMEJO by Jim Ross. Lonan Dunlee sees a rancher ambushed and vows to find the killers. In the search he unravels an elaborate scheme involving a false burial, a conniving brother, a corrupt lawman, and the vicious Gaster brothers. Number 2 in the Dunlee Westerns Series.

BRECK'S CHOICE by Bernard Palmer. Former gunman John Breck had sworn never to use a gun again. But when his gold is stolen and his wife and child murdered, he must find the killers. And his only clue is a broken hoofprint. Number 1 in the Breck Westerns Series.

HUNTED GUN by Bernard Palmer. Colorado rancher John Breck encounters an ambush, suspicious townspeople, and deceit spawned by gold fever as he searches for the killers of a rancher who just found gold. Number 2 in the Breck Westerns Series.

KID BRECKINRIDGE by Bernard Palmer. This tale introduces young John Breckinridge (the John Breck of *Breck's Choice* and *Hunted Gun*). John, a runaway, learns a lot about the Old West as he experiences an Indian ambush, a cattle drive, and a bank robbery. Number 3 in the Breck Westerns Series.

Other Living Books Best-sellers

LORD, YOU LOVE TO SAY YES by Ruth Harms Calkin. In this collection of prayer-poems the author speaks openly and honestly with her Lord about hopes and dreams, longings and frustrations, and her observations of life.   07-3824 $2.95.

MORE THAN A CARPENTER by Josh McDowell. A hard-hitting book for people who are skeptical about Jesus' deity, his resurrection, and his claims on their lives.   07-4552 $2.95.

NOW IS YOUR TIME TO WIN by Dave Dean. In this true-life story, Dean shares how he locked into seven principles that enabled him to bounce back from failure to success. Read about successful men and women—from sports and entertainment celebrities to the ordinary people next door—and discover how you too can bounce back from failure to success!   07-4727 $2.95.

THE POSITIVE POWER OF JESUS CHRIST by Norman Vincent Peale. All his life the author has been leading men and women to Jesus Christ. In this book he tells of his boyhood encounters with Jesus and of his spiritual growth as he attended seminary and began his world-renowned ministry.   07-4914 $3.95.

REASONS by Josh McDowell and Don Stewart. In a convenient question-and-answer format, the authors address many of the commonly asked questions about the Bible and evolution.   07-5287 $3.95.

ROCK by Bob Larson. A well-researched and penetrating look at today's rock music and rock performers, their lyrics, and their life-styles.   07-5686 $3.50.

SHAPE UP FROM THE INSIDE OUT by John R. Throop. Learn how to conquer the problem of being overweight! In this honest, often humorous book, Throop shares his own personal struggle with this area and how he gained fresh insight about the biblical relationship between physical and spiritual fitness.   07-5899 $2.95.

TAKE ME HOME by Bonnie Jamison. This touching, candid story of the author's relationship with her dying mother will offer hope and assurance to those dealing with an aging parent, relative, or friend.   07-6901 $3.50.

TELL ME AGAIN, LORD, I FORGET by Ruth Harms Calkin. You will easily identify with Calkin in this collection of prayer-poems about the challenges, peaks, and quiet moments of each day.   07-6990 $3.50.

THROUGH GATES OF SPLENDOR by Elisabeth Elliot. This unforgettable story of five men who braved the Auca Indians has become one of the most famous missionary books of all times.   07-7151 $3.95.

WAY BACK IN THE HILLS by James C. Hefley. The story of Hefley's colorful childhood in the Ozarks makes reflective reading for those who like a nostalgic journey into the past.   07-7821 $3.95.

Other Living Books Best-sellers

ANSWERS by Josh McDowell and Don Stewart. In a question-and-answer format, the authors tackle sixty-five of the most-asked questions about the Bible, God, Jesus Christ, miracles, other religions, and creation. 07-0021 $3.95.

THE BEST CHRISTMAS PAGEANT EVER by Barbara Robinson. A delightfully wild and funny story about what happens to a Christmas program when the "Horrible Herdman" brothers and sisters are miscast in the roles of the biblical Christmas story characters. 07-0137 $2.50.

BUILDING YOUR SELF-IMAGE by Josh McDowell. Here are practical answers to help you overcome your fears, anxieties, and lack of self-confidence. Learn how God's higher image of who you are can take root in your heart and mind. 07-1395 $3.95.

THE CHILD WITHIN by Mari Hanes. The author shares insights she gained from God's Word during her own pregnancy. She identifies areas of stress, offers concrete data about the birth process, and points to God's sure promises that he will "gently lead those that are with young." 07-0219 $2.95.

400 WAYS TO SAY I LOVE YOU by Alice Chapin. Perhaps the flame of love has almost died in your marriage. Maybe you have a good marriage that just needs a little "spark." Here is a book especially for the woman who wants to rekindle the flame of romance in her marriage; who wants creative, practical, useful ideas to show the man in her life that she cares. 07-0919 $2.50.

GIVERS, TAKERS, AND OTHER KINDS OF LOVERS by Josh McDowell and Paul Lewis. This book bypasses vague generalities about love and sex and gets right to the basic questions: Whatever happened to sexual freedom? What's true love like? Do men respond differently than women? If you're looking for straight answers about God's plan for love and sexuality, this book was written for you. 07-1031 $2.95.

HINDS' FEET ON HIGH PLACES by Hannah Hurnard. A classic allegory of a journey toward faith that has sold more than a million copies! 07-1429 $3.95.

LORD, COULD YOU HURRY A LITTLE? by Ruth Harms Calkin. These prayer-poems from the heart of a godly woman trace the inner workings of the heart, following the rhythms of the day and the seasons of the year with expectation and love. 07-3816 $2.95.

WHAT WIVES WISH THEIR HUSBANDS KNEW ABOUT WOMEN by James Dobson. The best-selling author of *DARE TO DISCIPLINE* and *THE STRONG-WILLED CHILD* brings us this vital book that speaks to the unique emotional needs and aspirations of today's woman. An immensely practical, interesting guide. 07-7896 $3.50.

Other Living Books Best-sellers

THE ANGEL OF HIS PRESENCE by Grace Livingston Hill. This book captures the romance of John Wentworth Stanley and a beautiful young woman whose influence causes John to reevaluate his well-laid plans for the future. 07-0047 $2.50.

HOW TO BE HAPPY THOUGH MARRIED by Tim LaHaye. One of America's most successful marriage counselors gives practical, proven advice for marital happiness. 07-1499 $3.50.

JOHN, SON OF THUNDER by Ellen Gunderson Traylor. In this saga of adventure, romance, and discovery, travel with John—the disciple whom Jesus loved—down desert paths, through the courts of the Holy City, to the foot of the cross. Journey with him from his luxury as a privileged son of Israel to the bitter hardship of his exile on Patmos. 07-1903 $4.95.

KAREN'S CHOICE by Janice Hermansen. College students Karen and Jon fall in love and are heading toward marriage when Karen discovers she is pregnant. Struggle with Karen and Jon through the choices they make and observe how they cope with the consequences and eventually find the forgiveness of Christ. 07-2027 $3.50.

LIFE IS TREMENDOUS! by Charlie "Tremendous" Jones. Believing that enthusiasm makes the difference, Jones shows how anyone can be happy, involved, relevant, productive, healthy, and secure in the midst of a high-pressure, commercialized society. 07-2184 $2.50.

LOOKING FOR LOVE IN ALL THE WRONG PLACES by Joe White. Using wisdom gained from many talks with young people, White steers teens in the right direction to find love and fulfillment in a personal relationship with God. 07-3825 $3.50.

LORD, I KEEP RUNNING BACK TO YOU by Ruth Harms Calkin. In prayer-poems tinged with wonder, joy, humanness, and questioning, the author speaks for all of us who are groping and learning together what it means to be God's child. 07-3819 $3.50.

SUCCESS: THE GLENN BLAND METHOD by Glenn Bland. The author shows how to set goals and make plans that really work. His ingredients of success include spiritual, financial, educational, and recreational balances. 07-6689 $3.50.

MOUNTAINS OF SPICES by Hannah Hurnard. Here is an allegory comparing the nine spices mentioned in the Song of Solomon to the nine fruits of the Spirit. A story of the glory of surrender by the author of *HINDS' FEET ON HIGH PLACES*. 07-4611 $3.50.

THE NEW MOTHER'S BOOK OF BABY CARE by Marjorie Palmer and Ethel Bowman. From what you will need to clothe the baby to how to know when to call the doctor, this book will give you all the basic knowledge necessary to be the parent your child needs. 07-4695 $2.95.

The books listed are available at your bookstore. If unavailable, send check with order to cover retail price plus $1.00 per book for postage and handling to:

Christian Book Service
Box 80
Wheaton, Illinois 60189

Prices and availability subject to change without notice. Allow 4–6 weeks for delivery.